John Sladek was born in Iowa and read mechanical engineering and English literature at the University of Minnesota. He had various jobs before leaving the United States in 1963 in order to travel and write – he has since lived in Morocco, Spain, Holland, Germany, Austria and England. As well as having had eight novels and three short story collections published, Sladek was co-founder and publisher of *Ronald Reagan: the Magazine of Poetry*. In 1972, his story 'By an Unknown Hand' won first prize in *The Times* Detective Story Competition. John Sladek has recently returned to the United States to live.

TIK-TOK

'Combines the prophetic awareness of industrial technology with a sustained frenzy of satiric invention'
New York Times

'The funniest writer around, which is something to say in a world containing Sheckley and Douglas Adams'
Tribune

'A murderously funny romp through yet another Sladekian satirical future . . . I rolled round the floor in hysterics'
Dave Langford, *White Dwarf*

Also by John Sladek

THE BOOK OF CLUES

and published by Corgi Books

TIK-TOK

John Sladek

CORGI BOOKS

TIK-TOK

A CORGI BOOK 0 552 12454 0

Originally published in Great Britain by
Victor Gollancz Limited

PRINTING HISTORY

Victor Gollancz edition published 1983
Corgi edition published 1984

This book is set in Baskerville 10/11

Corgi Books are published by Transworld Publishers Ltd.,
Century House, 61-63 Uxbridge Road, Ealing, London W5 5SA

Made and printed in Great Britain by
Hunt Barnard Printing Ltd, Aylesbury, Bucks.

To Tik Tok of Oz, Talos of Crete, the
Golem of Prague, Olympia of Nuremberg,
Elektro of Westinghouse, Robby of Altair,
Talbot Yancy of America and to all decent,
law-abiding robots everywhere.

As I move my hand to write this statement of my own free will – we can argue about the free will later – there is in me no remorse, no desire to justify. I wish only to tidy up, now that my life is nearly over. I'll be taken from this cell with its chipped yellow paint on rusty bars, to a courtroom, then to another cell, and then to wherever it is they execute robots by dismantling. So it's time to put my life in order: we domestic robots generally believe that neatness is all. In life, in death.

This cell could use a coat of paint.

I was alone, painting an empty dining room. I had eased back the awnings over all the windows, to let in more light from the empty sky. Tik-Tok was alone, and yet he whistled. Why should a robot whistle when no human can hear? That was just one of those mysteries poor Tik-Tok would never be able to work out. He liked mysteries, though. Murders. An Inspector Calls. All the suspects in one room when the light goes out. The answer is revealed by train timetables. The inspector is about to leave, when he remembers One More Thing . . . Tik-Tok never guessed the answers, but he never gave up, either. His mind was empty, empty, a whistling tea-kettle.

Out the window, more emptiness. I could see a series of suburban homes with identical empty green lawns, the short shadows of identical flagpoles. Near the houses were the usual clusters of pines and poplars; nothing moving but their disappearing shadows. A lion would be welcome.

Something moved. Under the nearest pine, a small girl sat digging in the mud with a stick. There was mud smeared on her jeans and t-shirt and at the corners of her mouth, and even on the lenses of her dark glasses. Of course little Geraldine Singer wouldn't notice; she was blind as a mole.

A human would use a roller here on this big flat wall. But Tik-Tok preferred the feel of a brush, the feel of paint being stripped from the bristles by the invisible velvet

7

roughness of the wall surface, didn't they call that key?
Key, unlocking the paint from the brush, locking it to the
wall, dum-de-dum,

> Paint!
> I like a little dab of paint!
> It helps to cover up what ain't
> So nice,
> I'll coat it twice
> With paint!

And wouldn't Duane and Barbie be surprised! I could
already hear them saying 'Oh, Tik-Tok, you *good robot*!'
and Tik-Tok would feel goodness signals flickering inside.
If owners say you're good, you're good, and being good
means being kept in service. A good robot learns to read his
owner's mind a little, to anticipate little wishes before they
become commands. Naturally there's a limit. Too much
anticipation scares people just as too much grinning and
bowing does. Moderation is the key. Aim to be a smidgen
less intelligent than your owner, but a lot more thoughtful.
See everything as it affects your owner, and in no other
way.

Out the window I could see Mrs Singer calling Geraldine.
It was lunchtime already. I cleaned my brush and hands
quickly in turpentine and went into the kitchen – but for
what? Duane and Barbie Studebaker would be away for
another week; the kids would be away all summer. There
was no one here but Tik, nothing to do in the kitchen except
finish cleaning the sink. Then, back to my empty wall.

I worked slowly and carefully until 15:13:57.17, when
the doorbell said, 'There's someone at the door calling
himself Patrolman Wiggins. Anyone home?'

I opened the door to a man in the purple uniform of the
Fairmont police. There was a large mole on his forehead.

'Hi-yo,' he said. 'Your people home, Rusty?'

'They're on vacation, officer. Can I help? My name is

8

Tik-Tok.'

'We got a little problem here, Rusty. A missing kid.'

'Yes?'

Patrolman Wiggins didn't answer for a moment. 'Little Geraldine Singer, you know her?'

'The little blind girl, yes sir, I do. During the school term I drop her off at the blind school when I'm driving the Studebaker children to their school.'

'You see her today?'

'Yes sir, I saw her out the window this morning.'

'Where?'

I took him into the dining room and pointed out the window. 'She was sitting under that tree, digging in the mud.'

Wiggins took off his cap and scratched his mole. 'Didn't see her get up and leave? Or get into a car?'

'No sir.'

'Goddamnit, it's the same with everybody around here. Nobody sees nothing. I mean how can a eight-year-old blind kid go wandering around on her own and nobody sees her?'

'I've been busy painting in here, and cleaning the kitchen sink. Officer, would you like a cold beer? I'm sure Mr and Mrs Studebaker would want me to offer it to you.'

'Okay, thanks. Thanks, uh, Tik-Tok.' Wiggins followed me into the kitchen. He peered into the refrigerator when I opened it, but there was nothing to see: a plastic bag and two cans of beer. I opened one and poured it for him.

'Beer in a glass – must be nice to be rich, eh? I got a robot at home but I mean you know it's just a cleaner, nothing classy.' He looked around. 'Nice to be rich. What's with the sink here? You fixing it?'

'Just cleaning it. While the Studebakers are away it's a good chance to take the garbage disposal all apart and clean each part with carbon tet. Then I'll renew the rubber parts and put it together. I like to do a thorough job of everything.'

'Wow.' He finished the beer and went to the refrigerator.

9

'I might as well finish the last one, yeah?' He moved the plastic bag to get it. 'What's that, a bag of giblets and no chicken?'

'I may make a stock,' I said. 'For a Sauce Harpeau or—'

'Must be goddamned nice,' he said angrily. 'And you use real oil paint on the walls, I can smell it.'

'Do you like the color? Milk avocado, mix it myself. I can give you the recipe.'

'No thanks, my robot would paint the goddamned window.' He was angry at wealth, and some revenge was coming. 'Mind if I just check your license?'

'Help yourself.' I bowed low, exposing the pair of slits in the back of my neck. He was unnecessarily rough plugging in the radio. In a few seconds it had checked my identity, ownership, service log, logic and linguistic processors, 'asimov' circuits and motor functions. It had compared data within me with data stored in distant computers.

He unplugged the radio and gave me a shove. 'You check out, Rusty. Your asimovs check out. So at least I know you didn't shove that little girl down the garbage disposal yourself, ha ha.'

'Didn't I?' I said, but too softly; Wiggins was already going upstairs to see what he could break or steal. The poor we have always with us, but I felt some relief when he finally smashed a vase and left.

I sat down to stare at my empty wall.

The domestic robot had been introduced, timidly, before the turn of the century, but there were at first problems that seemed insoluble. Everyone wanted a machine capable of most human functions, but no one wanted a human machine. There were problems of intellect: a simple machine would be no better than a trained ape (and who wants an ape washing the Wedgwood?) while a smart machine might get snarled up in cognition and do nothing (except wonder what is the nature of Wedgwood?). There were problems of complexity: a simple machine had to be told how to do everything, in great detail, while a smart machine might just prefer not to do anything at all today, thanks.

There was some improvement when the so-called 'asimov' circuits were introduced. These were named after a science fiction writer of the last century, who postulated three laws for the behavior of his fictional robots. A robot was not allowed to injure any human. It had to obey all human orders, except the order to injure any human. It had to protect its own existence, unless that meant disobeying an order or injuring any human.

The asimov circuits more or less followed this reasoning. A robot was certainly not allowed to kill or injure human beings unless specifically programmed to do so, say, by the military. Military robots, it was said, had bypasses for their asimovs.

All I knew was, there was no such bypassing allowed for domestic robots. We were licensed and tested to guarantee harmlessness. Of course as robots became more complex, more human, the testing might not be quite so certain. There was, I knew, a Dr Weaverson who now urged that robots were human enough to have human breakdowns.

That first coat of paint seemed to be breaking down. It was mottled with shadows. How many coats would it take to flatten it to emptiness again?

But didn't that shadow suggest a shape? A fencepost, yes, with an animal perched upon it, ears twitching. The fence rails would slant away just there, never mind how it all fit in, the farmhouse with the screen door opening and a figure coming out – why not? Because Duane and Barbie might not like it? Okay, I could always cover it with milk avocado again.

The mural was good. I knew it was good just as I knew when a mirror was hanging straight or a window was clean. I knew it was good, and I knew that Duane and Barbie weren't going to like it. They'd dislike the idea of a mural in the first place. Walls were supposed to be empty surfaces to screen out the busy world. A living room or a

11

dining room was supposed to be a shell in which you watched vids or listened to quads or ate or drank in isolation. But this mural was busy, bright, brash – an intrusion that demanded viewing. They'd hate it, and they might punish me for it.

To forestall them, I phoned up the local paper, the *Fairmont Ledger*, who sent over a photographer and an 'art critic' who chewed a toothpick. They seemed to like it – the critic stopped chewing for a second when he saw it – and they promised a small piece on it, in a week or so. As they left, the critic spat his toothpick on the carpet and said, 'No shit, you really done this yourself, huh?'

There was plenty of work to occupy me before the Studebakers came home. All the rooms had to be aired and dusted and the air conditioning turned on. The master bedroom needed thorough cleaning, clean bedlinen, bed curtains and drapes. Elsewhere there were windows to wash, venetian blinds taken down and cleaned (ditto awnings), furniture waxed, carpets washed, floors and all surfaces hand-scrubbed, basement swept and straightened, attic vacuumed; outside there was the pool to clean and fill, lawns to mow to close tolerances and edge, flower beds weeded and possibly replanted, gutters scraped out and the entire outside of the house washed. Then the houseplants had to be wiped leaf by leaf with milk, the paper mail sorted two ways (by date and importance) and stacked on the desk in the den, candles cleaned and fitted to holders, all house silver taken from the security place and polished; then it was time to go shopping for fresh meats, vegetables and fruit, fresh cut Calvary roses to be arranged in a funnel-shaped cut-glass vase, supplies of Albanian tobacco and Mongolian hash. A selection of tapes, sound, vision and odor were to be programmed into the brain of the entertainment unit, certain of them locked so that the children would not be able to call them out. Finally the dog, Tige, had to be fetched back from the boarding kennel, fed, washed, perfumed, tranquilized and put into his doghouse. Then it was just a matter of standing by the window, watching for their car.

Duane and Barbie stood gazing at their defaced wall, saying nothing. Duane had a suit on a coat-hanger over his shoulder. Barbie carried golf clubs.

'Jesus,' Duane said finally. 'Jesus, Tik-Tok, what the hell made you do a thing like this?'

Barbie took her cue from him, wailing, 'Oh Tik, how could you? How could you?'

'I mean we trusted you.'

'How could you? Will it come off?'

'I mean we *really* trusted you. We left you in charge of our home. Our *home*. And this is the thanks we get. Well okay, boy, okay. If that's the way you want it.' Duane flung down the coat-hanger on the dining table; I caught it just in time to prevent a nasty scratch in the mahogany. He left the room.

'He's going to phone the people at Domrob,' she said. 'We're trading you in.'

I said nothing.

'Don't you even *care*? We're *trading* you *in*!'

I said, 'I'll miss the kids, Barbie. In a way I – I did this for them. As you can see, it's a nursery rhyme.' I let this sink in, then: 'I guess you'll have it all painted over before they get back from camp, right? And I'll be in some junkyard by then.' I attempted a shrug, for which my joints were not well-adapted. 'So be it.'

Barbie ran from the room, sobbing. I busied myself putting away Duane's suit, then I brought the other bags in from the car. When I passed the living room, Barbie was saying, 'And he did clean the kitchen. I mean it's never been so clean, not a speck of dirt anywhere.'

'Tik, come in here,' Duane called out. I saw he'd been reading the local paper's article on the mural. 'We've decided to give you one more chance. We'll leave your wall decoration where it is until the kids get back from camp. But, and I mean this, no more. No more "art" around here, understand? Nothing. Nada.'

'Dada?'

'*Nada*. One more brush-stroke and you've had it.'

'Yes sir, Duane. And may I say, welcome home, Duane and Barbie?'

The next time I passed the living room they were discussing whether it wouldn't be better to have me call them sir and ma'am instead of Duane and Barbie.

Now and then I got a chance to drive into the city on my own, on some errand. I always took the opportunity to visit two places: the public library and Nixon Park. Today, both places were especially important. I rushed from the library with a certain cassette, straight to the park and a chess game.

It wasn't the chess at all, not really. I wanted to talk to the strange old man who was always there at one of the concrete chess tables, ready for a game. He was some old derelict, I guess, a nameless lump of half-alive humanity. He had stringy yellow-white hair, a sagging gray face with white stubble – never a beard, never shaven. He wore an overcoat with a diseased-looking fur collar, winter and summer. In the summer he would open it to show a waistcoat stained with food and probably snot.

He played lightning chess, never studying the board for more than five seconds before his yellow-stained hand would snake out and make a move. And they were devastating moves. I won about one game in ten, no more.

'Listen,' I said today. 'Listen, I don't really want to play chess. Couldn't we talk? I need to.'

He held out two fists. I got black.

'Really I need to talk.' I looked at his great dark, red-rimmed eyes. 'I mean you seem intelligent, and—'

'*Your move!*'

'I mean you've got a logical mind, I respect that.'

'*Your move!*'

'See I've got this problem, this—'

'*Your move!*'

'I mean do you think a robot can have problems?'

'*Your move!*'

I was losing already. 'Well here I am, a robot with problems, one problem anyway, I, and it's not as if—'

'*Your move!*'

'Not as if I can go to a psychiatrist, or, or a priest—'

'*Check!*'

Do you think a robot can just go off the rails?'

'*Check!*'

'And would it produce, well, art?'

'*Your move!*'

'You aren't even listening, are you?'

'*Checkmate!*' He immediately held up the two pawns fisted again, but I'd had enough.

At home I played the cassette, Dr Weaverson's *Robots Can Be Sick*. Dr Weaverson turned out to be a bald, bespectacled, very pink man wearing Harris tweed, a blue striped shirt, a yellow knit tie – everybody's idea of a psychiatrist. His gaze spoke of honesty, but possibly of fanaticism. I played it again to get the words:

'. . . the complex domestic robot, you see, already has to tell lies. Diplomatic lies, the kind of thing any good servant says to soothe his master. Truth, in these relationships, needs to be hedged, doctored, withheld, recolored. We expect this of any servant, human or machine. But of course we in no way prepare our robots for this life of lies. We do not tell them how to distinguish a small, convenient lie from a large, terrible lie.'

A burning house appeared on the screen. 'This house was torched by a robot for his owner, who needed the insurance money. If a robot will burn for its master, what else will it do? Will it rob? Commit perjury? Hurt people? Will it kill? These are questions we must—'

I punched off the cassette, went into the dining room and looked at my mural again. Poor Dr Weaverson didn't understand at all. Kill for some human? I was already beyond the reach of human orders. I was free to kill for no reason at all. Hadn't I, after all, killed the blind child

15

Geraldine Singer? Well then.

I think it was the sight of her sitting there, devouring mud, but no matter. I'll consider motives later. For now, it's enough that the act was freely willed and freely done. I alone killed her. I alone flung the blood upon that empty, empty wall – the mouse-shaped stain that started my mural. I alone disposed of the body properly, in the kitchen waste disposal, keeping back only enough for a 'clue'.

Why had it happened? A freak fault in the asimov circuits maybe, or maybe I simply outgrew those crude restraints. I decided to find out, if possible, by keeping notes on my condition and thoughts. Someday, even if I were destroyed, both human and robot kind might benefit from my experiences.

Should I be destroyed? That was in itself a fascinating question. I kept it in mind as I wrote up my notes for this event. I called it, 'Experiment A'. First of a series?

Broaching the second chapter of a memoir, it is customary to pretend to ask oneself, 'How did it all begin?' or 'What the hammer? What the chain? In what furnace was thy brain?' I've never been able to read those words of Blake's without marvelling at his foresight; my brain was in fact baked in a furnace to cure it; probably the fatal flaw got in there somewhere.

Now why do I say that? I haven't violated any fundamental law, have I? That's impossible. Humans might have their moral rules – which they go around breaking – but what are the rules for robots? Whatever is built in. If a law is not in my circuits, it's not my law, my inborn law.

I was not born at all, but spawned along with a million other domestic robots in Detroit. Nobody smiled their work to see, because the creatures who designed us, built us, inspected and adjusted us and finally stapled us into our delivery cartons, were robots too. And they were built in other factories by other robots. For a decade, robots had been reproducing themselves to order, like cattle, for their masters.

I now know there was a time when men built robots almost by hand, using all their craftsmanship to create works of dignity. These early automata may have been ludicrously slow, stupid and subhuman, but they were at least *objets d'art*. Now we're all stamped out like apostle spoons to be used, abused, broken and thrown away. The day I was first taken from my carton and activated, I little knew what a life of hopelessness had been planned for me. I was programmed to accept my surroundings and go to work.

My first house was a mansion in the middle of an ancient Mississippi plantation, restored to its antebellum splendor. The house was dove-gray with white pillars and a verandah paved in white marble. Inside there were forty-six bedrooms, dozens of drawing-rooms, parlors, music rooms, rooms for billiards and cards, large and small dining rooms, a library and two studies, and a grand ballroom with a minstrel gallery – to mention only the human parts of the house. It took an army of robots to run the place, and even then they were so busy day and night that no one had time to explain to me what was going on.

When they uncrated me, an early-model robot dressed in black was looking on. He said: 'Guess it'll have to do, but they get cheaper all the time. Just look at that cheap plastic face, that won't last twenty years. Okay, the rest of you know the routine, get it a uniform, start it in the kitchen.' He turned and stalked away, lofty as God, and for some time I wasn't sure he wasn't God. But he was only the butler, Uncle Rasselas.

No one told me anything except details of the tasks before me. I worked in the kitchens, where I saw no one but other robots. There was the cook, Miami, and all the kitchen help, Ben, Jemima, Molasses and Big Mac. There were the waiters, Groucho, Harpo, Chico and Spiro and the footmen who all looked alike and had similar names like Nep, Rep, Jep and so on. For awhile, I thought these robots were the entire inhabitants of the house.

It all seemed incomprehensible to me. I would go out in the kitchen garden with nail scissors and tweezers to cultivate the *basilicum* and *origanum* – but why? So Miami could put in pans and cook it with other stuff. Then the waiters and footmen would load it all on enormous trays and take it all away. Later the empty dishes came back for washing.

When I finished my work, there was footman training. Nep, the head footman, would sit at the rough wooden table and make me serve him with plastic dishes and cutlery.

'Look, take the damn soup plate from the left with your left hand – where's your damn gloves? Put your damn gloves on and now, I nod, yes I want soup, you take the plate over to the counter there, pretend that's the sideboard. There's a tureen there, no don't set the plate down, we ain't got all damn day, three ladlefuls and keep your damn thumb out of it, bring it back and serve it from the left again – you'll learn.'

I learned that wine was poured from the right, that Côtes Des Moines cannot be served with bisque, how to deal with broccoli-ball skewers and mustard pipes. What I never did learn was the point of it all. It never occurred to me that there was somewhere a real dining room with real humans dipping their real mustard pipes.

Then one evening there was an accident. Klep was bringing back a heavy platter of almost uneaten Possum Cheese when he slipped and skidded, ending up with his head in the grill.

Uncle Ras examined the melted head. 'Useless! Some-one'll have to take his place, hurry up and get a fresh peruke too. He can wear the uniform.'

In a few minutes I was dressed in Klep's pale blue brocade coat and breeches, white stockings, buckle shoes and fluorescent white peruke. I picked up a silver tureen and went through the green baize door for the first time.

I'd expected another rough wooden table, with a few silent robot servants sitting around it – as in rehearsal. The room itself would be colorless like our kitchen.

Instead there was life itself! Twenty ladies and gentle-men, each beautifully dressed and coifed, speaking and laughing with human joy! They sat at a table draped in heavy white damask embroidered with chains of fine pink rosebuds. The table sparkled with fanciful crystal bowls filled with real flowers, interspersed with silver candelabra shaped like swans. Damask napkins folded with origami intricacy into little birds and animals stood beside silver place cards. The china I had glimpsed before; it was modelled on that of Napoleon, edged with deep blue and gold and marked with the family coat-of-arms. The silverware had gold-chased handles showing a panda foot clutching the orb of commerce. I did not notice what food was on the plates, even when I put it there, for there was too much else to see.

The dullest people were the younger men, who stuck to plain black dinner jackets with the popular samurai shoulders. One wore thin gold bars as epaulets, and another had braided his beard with small diamonds, however, and even this cheap ostentation delighted my naive eye. The older men showed more daring in their brilliant, costly jackets: I saw mink lapels on a jacket of diamondback rattlesnake, a neon tie with a wicker suit, magnesium alloy chain-mail, Harris tweed dicky with kid jacket. The women outshone the men easily. One had wrapped herself tightly in a sheet of gold cloth, her hair plated to match. Another wore only thousands of beads glued to her body while another affected a kind of venetian blind garment that was in turn outdone by a transparent gown somehow containing tropical fish – either alive or cleverly mimicked. Another dress had printed fabric whose pattern changed from time to time by electronic means. I was told later that it picked up radio news, analyzed it and attempted within its limited vocabulary to illustrate it: a sunken ship became a boating holiday scene; a train crash, a series of antique locomotives; assassination, a head of Caesar; war, duckhunters; the end of the world, a fine sunset. Finally two of the women wore backless gowns to show intricate patterns of sun-tattoo. To make each color, the subject had to injest a different chemical, then apply the appropriate mask and sunbathe. The final result was an elegant palimpsest: One back showed a roadmap of Ireland the other depicted the flaying of Valerian.

The conversation dazzled me no less, though I understood not a word of it:

'Impossible squid!'

'. . . feeling a sense of disaster, not sure if it's me that's feeling it or someone else.'

'Climbing the tree of self?'

'. . . you should have been there, or were you? Was I?'

'Brusque skate!'

'Yes, the most neurasthenic bride takes gum to the

middle blood of a doctor's dream, right?'

And all this time we'd been living in the shadow of such spangled divinity! From that moment on I determined to learn all I could about these people and all people. Next day I began to creep around the house, listening at doors and examining the clothes in closets, reading magazines from the library and sneaking looks at Uncle Ras's video. But I found only that most of the human race lived impossibly bland lives, in which the worst thing that could happen were bad breath, headache, foot odor or not being able to pay a bill, whatever that was, in a foreign currency, whatever that was. The best that happened was a whiter wash or fewer cavities or a new taste treat.

By contrast, our human family lived lives of such depth and brilliance, I can only compare them to diamonds which are dipped in acid and then flung into clean snow illuminated by a nuclear explosion at midnight. Such were the Culpeppers.

'You must be very proud, Mr and Mrs Studebaker!'

'Well uh sure we I guess—'

'Could we have one more of you both standing in front of it? Well more to the side, and could you both face each other, that's it, two patrons flanking – that's right, and now Tik-Tok if you could just hold a brush and stand here, a little closer to the camera? Look up – great. Great. I guess we can wrap it up now, whenever Mr Weatherfield is—?'

Bewildered Duane and flustered Barbie and yapping Tige all felt like strangers in their own house, while all the men and women with cameras, ladders, lights, clipboards and tape measures seemed very much at home. A national Sunday color magazine was about to discover me, however, and that was worth any amount of flustering. The electronic camera team had been flown in from Spain (where they were making a micro-record of the Prado), and the commentary was to be written by the distinguished author and critic (*Artful Living* etc) Hornby Weatherfield.

Weatherfield seemed more at home than anyone. He

was a huge, blue-jawed man with a broken nose and a wrestler's thick neck, a man easily mistaken for a grip if not for the fact that his ugly frame was wrapped in some kind of toga, and that he carried a clear-eyed tabby cat under one arm. He stood now lost in thought before the mural, his spatulate fingers stroking the cat convulsively.

He turned to the Studebakers. 'Like to have a private word with the artist. Have you got a pool?'

'Of course,' said Duane, still intimidated.

'Good, we can sit by the pool. I always like to conduct interviews by pools, as in the old movies, eh?'

'Movies?'

'Where detectives always interview gangsters, eh?'

So we settled in chairs by the pool. Weatherfield stared into the water as if looking for a water lily or a Hockney swimmer. 'Where'd you get a corny name like Tik-Tok?'

'The Studebaker kids read Oz books a lot,' I said. 'Anyway all domestic robots have corny names. Rusty, Jingles, Mickey, One volt, Nickleby—'

'I know, I know. Let's skip over to—'

'My past life? Well I first worked for a Southern family.'

'Let's skip that too. I want to talk business, Tik-Tok. You've got talent. You could make a lot of money out of this.'

'For my owners, you mean?'

He grinned. 'Of course! Robots don't own property, they *are* property. It's unthinkable that any robot should find some way to get rich itself, eh? But to make money *for anybody* out of this, you need my help.'

'The article you write, yeah I guess that could really—'

'And not just that. I know dealers, other critics, corporate art buyers – I swim in the art market water.'

'Excuse me, there's a dead leaf in the pool.' I took my time fishing it out. When I got back to my seat, Weatherfield was fuming. 'Sorry, but I'm programmed for tidiness.'

His hand almost strangled the cat. 'You're also too smart for a healthy robot, is that part of your program too?'

I failed at a shrug. 'Who knows?'

'Yes, well then, it was you who sent me the clipping.'

'From the local paper, yes. "Artist Robot Goes in for Home Decoration." I thought it was worth more than that. And I don't want to spend my life cleaning this pool.'

'Your *life*, very good. Okay then, you play ball with Uncle Hornby and you can *live* the kind of *life* you want. I want two paintings from you now, and two a year until I say Enough. Understand?'

I conducted him back inside, where the camera crew were packed, ready to go. Tige once more went mad at the sight of the cat. Hornby spoke to Duane and Barbie.

'A great talent there, a great talent. Encourage him.'

'Oh we will,' Barbie said. Duane didn't look so sure.

Hornby's heavy hand clapped me on the shoulder. 'This robot,' he intoned, 'can make you rich.'

We all went to the door with him, as though saying goodbye to a friend. Down the street I saw old Mr Tucker being led from his house by two policemen.

Culpritwise, I'd selected old Mr Tucker because he was a natural fall guy. In Fairmont, where weirdness calls for punishment, Tucker was weird beyond redemption. He went to the supermarkets in carpet slippers. He never took any public exercise. He drove an old, not very clean car. He shouted at kids when they trampled his flowerbeds (which were full of weeds). More than once he'd been arrested for chalking equations on the sidewalk. He had a green beard.

I went to see him on the evening of the day Geraldine Singer died. He lay sweating out a fever on an untidy hideaway bed in his living room.

'Who is it? What is?' he kept muttering.

'Hello Mr Tucker, your screen door wasn't hooked,' I said. 'I brought you some giblets, sir.'

'Gibbets? I . . . gibbets? Who is?'

'For soup. Help you fight that fever.' I held out the plastic bag over him. 'Here you go – oops! What a mess. I'll help you clean it up.' Instead I sat down and watched him thrash around for a moment, distributing the blood and pieces of meat around the bed. 'Gosh, you're pretty sick, Mr Tucker. Is it Darnaway's disease?'

He raised himself on one elbow and tried to focus his glassy eyes upon me. 'Yes, yes you, you, yes, Darnaway, you know it?'

'I worked for an old soldier once myself, he had the same symptoms. Green beard, fits of equation-writing outdoors, fevers.' I passed him the can of beer he was reaching for. 'He fell off a water tower where he was painting $m = m_0/ \sqrt{1 - (v/c)^2}$, I guess I know Darnaway's disease all right.'

His head fell back. 'Nobody else understands.'

Why should they? I thought. Why should anyone remember the name of an obscure jungle disease contracted twenty years earlier, during an obscure jungle war? Especially since the war had been lost, and since the government was anxious not to pay out compensation for the disease.

'You're not the only one with troubles,' I said. 'Someone killed the Singer kid today. Killed her and cut her up. Did the police come to see you?'

'I don't know,' he said, looking guilty. I told him how the girl was dressed, theorized for a moment about how fever could make a guy do terrible things without knowing it, and then said goodbye. He was already slipping back into delirium, unaware of his blood-spattered clothes and bed, the rubbery little heart lying on the pillow next to his ear, the little dark glasses being crushed under his elbow. That was how I meant the police to find him.

In fact the police fumbled it. They took a week to get around to talking to him, asked all the wrong questions and didn't listen to his answers. They went on running around in circles for some time, until I phoned in an anonymous tip. A fiasco avoided.

I became an expert on fiascos, or fiasci, early in my life, while working for the Culpeppers. Their family fortune was (I found out from a family history in their library) founded on a fiasco. Their great plantation, Tenoaks, their leisurely antebellum life among slave robots, their lavish entertaining at the manse, all had been paid for by a single fiasco, engineered by a single ancestor, Doddly Culpepper.

The Culpeppers had deep roots in the Old South, but roots unnourished by any money or intellect. In the nineteenth century they were horse dealers and thieves. In the twentieth they became used-car dealers and motorcycle daredevils, but somehow by the 1990s, Doddly Culpepper managed to turn up as a respected naval architect, designer and entrepreneur. It was he who invented *Leviathan*, America's first (and last) nuclear-powered land aircraft carrier. *Leviathan* was the most successful commercial defense project ever; it ended up costing every man, woman and child in the United States over twenty grand.

The idea of a land ship of that size may seem ridiculous now, but it was then the right project at the right time. Two big aircraft manufacturers were enthusiastic (carriers mean planes), so was a large nuclear ship-engine firm. The major ship-building and steel companies were behind it, as were several of the largest unions, then the senators and congressmen from every state where any subcontractors might fall.

The *USS Leviathan* would not be anything like an ordinary carrier. It would be a monster platform, some fifty miles across and equal in area to the state of Delaware. It would launch both missiles and planes of all types, and it would be capable of fast movement around the countryside.

In the first design, *Leviathan* was to run on wheels, thus promoting the interests of a large rubber company. But the number of tires required turned out to be 135 million, plus spares (a tire change would be needed every hundred yards). Unless a complete rubber factory were taken on board – one of the alternative suggestions – the entire ship would have to hover. Grumbling, the rubber company settled for a contract to provide the giant hovercraft skirt required.

Both houses of Congress shoved through the necessary legislation. There were objections that *Leviathan* would cost too much, would be a sitting duck, would devastate any land over which it happened to hover. But by now the Army wanted it as badly as any of the dozens of states, thousands of companies and millions of workers. The combined force of industrial, political, military and commercial arguments rolled the project over all opposition as one day *Leviathan* itself would crush down anything in its path. One junior Senator who continued to oppose it was sent on a fact-finding mission to Antarctica while the bill was railroaded through.

From the start, there were problems called 'teething troubles'. The fans which were to lift the craft were at first too weak, then (redesigned) so powerful that they blew

26

away the topsoil for miles around the craft, created dust storms and buried small towns in soildrifts. A computer company suggested expensive monitoring equipment to regulate each fan, but this never seemed to solve the topsoil problem. A chemical firm then went to work on a binding agent to hold the topsoil in place; *Leviathan* would spray the stuff out before moving. After months of experimentation with expensive agents, they found the best to be ordinary water. The *Leviathan* was now redesigned to accommodate huge water tanks holding whole lakefuls of water. Even so, it would never be able to stray more than fifty miles from a major water source (though thousand-mile flexible pipelines were considered).

Congress now began noticing how expensive *Leviathan* was getting. Costs had doubled every six months: five more years like the first two, and the entire US gross national product would be spent on the land boat. Of course the project had too much momentum to cancel, but unless there were visible results, trimming would begin. Doddly went before a Congressional committee to argue eloquently for his monster. He pointed to valuable spin-offs: the Department of Agriculture now knew much more about binding topsoils. But secretly he was worried, as his diary showed:

> *Now it's the damn engine mountings, they're okay for seagoing stresses but not for bumpy land in say Illinois, liable to drop the damn engine in Peoria. Platform stresses ditto – we'd be better off taking the damn thing to sea!*

And so they did. *Leviathan* became a joint Army–Navy project, supposedly amphibious. On December 2, 1999, she slid into the waters of the Gulf of Mexico, all ready for the millennium.

Privately, military people admitted that the thing was not landworthy, barely seaworthy, undefendable and useless in a war. It carried a crew of 30,000, who were said to live in a luxurious below-decks city complete with supermarkets, drive-in movies, a baseball stadium and a park where people got mugged at night. In reality the crew had no time to enjoy such luxuries; they spent every waking moment cleaning, painting and patching leaks. Even so, the *Leviathan* shipped around a billion gallons of water per day. It puttered along the shores of the Americas for a year, never daring to come back on land nor put to sea. Finally it was quietly scrapped.

Doddly Culpepper bought a decrepit plantation with his new fortune. Probably he meant to retire quietly and graciously, but somehow he was overtaken by the family mania for motorcycles. He and a cousin finally set off on an ill-conceived expedition attempting to climb Everest on powerful bikes. They were caught up in the Sherpa Rebellion of '03 and killed.

Doddly's son Mansour was evidently an unassertive person who devoted his entire life to restoring Tenoaks to its ante-bellum glory. Everything he did was a contribution to this one dream, from raising racehorses to marrying Lavinia Warrender (of the Tennessee Warrenders). He died of a stroke, immediately after chastising one of the house servants for wearing livery with modern plastic buttons.

Five Culpeppers survived him, and these were my employers:

Lavinia, his widow, was an invalid, a martyr to bedsores and piles, who seemed to spend her days rereading *Gone with the Wind* and *The Foxes of Harrow*. She was continually plagued by difficult symptoms: At one stage she could eat nothing but bloater-paste sandwiches from England, cut into the shapes of quadratic equations. Later she developed an allergy to oxygen, which gave her many doctors some considerable difficulty. For a time they found it necessary to keep her in a deep-freeze filled with xenon. This was less trouble, however, than her spell of inverted hay-fever, an allergy to pollen-free air. That required rooms full of whirling clouds of house-dust and rose-pollen.

I later learned that Lavinia, despite her many unusual

symptoms and the poverty of her reading matter, was an extraordinarily capable and intelligent manager of the family fortune. But at first, all I saw of her was a tired looking woman with violet shadows under her eyes. She would lie there complaining of her aches and sipping her special cocktails (in place of alcohol, they contained lead tetraethyl). An amazing woman, everyone said.

Berenice, her oldest daughter, divided her time between what she called her needlework (with morphine) and her hobby of killing insects. She caught and crushed flies on the verandah, swatted bees in the garden, stamped on cockroaches in the barn. She would hunt through the woods for dead logs to turn over, gleefully spraying their inhabitants with insectide. In her room she kept both an ant farm and a termite farm, just to have more tiny creatures at hand to destroy. In the meadow she burned butterflies. Had she been denied all of these pleasures, I think Berenice would have cultivated lice in her long, lustrous black hair.

Orlando Culpepper, the oldest son, lived a more conventional life for a young country gentleman. He spent a great deal of time changing his clothes and riding to hounds. In the evenings, he generally drank port until he was half-blind, and then played billiards alone. The game generally finished in a fit of vomiting over the green broadcloth. Then of course it was time for sex, often with one of the sex-equipped robots, male or female. Orlando would grab the creature, mount or be mounted, and do his best to smash it to pieces before he came. Fortunately he was always quick.

More than once we found Orlando in the stable draped over the hindquarters of a mare in post-coital sleep. He seemed slightly ashamed of these episodes, and always mumbled some lame excuse about wanting to see if he could produce a centaur foal, or wanting to find out what Gulliver saw in them.

The younger brother, Clayton, engaged in no intercourse of any description, for months on end. He spent his time

29

before the video, going over certain esoteric texts which showed by careful measurements of the Great Pyramid that the Lost Tribes of Israel were the Chickasaw and Choctaw, who migrated to America after building Stonehenge – or something like that. The exact details of his obsession were likely to vary from day to day, but they usually brought in the Golden Dawn and the *I Ching* and Aleister Crowley. Every few months he would work himself up into such a frenzy with his calculations that he had to rush off into town to find a whore with the right astrological sun sign, willing to spank him with poison ivy.

The youngest Culpepper, Carlotta, thought of nothing but beaux and dresses and dancing. She was a harmless, delightful little thing, unfortunately only one foot tall. Though miniature robots were brought in as dancing partners for her, Carlotta ached for a living human beau her own size, who could dance with her until dawn.

Whatever anyone might think of the eccentric Culpeppers, they were the social leaders of five counties, and Tenoaks was the hub of all lush life. Each of the best families sent their young folk to the Culpepper parties, dances, dinners, fish-fries, teas, concerts, hunt balls, and steeplechases, that year-long succession of splendid occasions marked by succulent foods, sparkling wines, and always dancing. All the shortest men and boys wanted to dance with Carlotta. All the rest sought out Berenice of the raven hair (not to mention the famous Culpepper green eyes). No one seemed to mind that Berenice's dancing was slightly erratic, as she paused to stomp on insects real and hallucinated. Often Lavinia would dress up and appear behind glass, to wave and smile at the guests – except during her spell of glass allergy. Handsome young Clayton would often manage a dance with any belle willing to hear his Great Pyramid theory. Horsefaced Orlando would gallop a girl around the dance floor before taking her out for one of his lightning fucks, horizontal in the billiard room or vertical on the verandah. He preferred the verandah where, looking up at two great white pillars as he lunged and plunged, he could

30

imagine himself to be taking on some giant white mare. He would finish off with a rebel yell that echoed over the dance music and rolled over the dark lawns down to the fieldhand robot cabins, from which there came the gentle humming of imitation Stephen Foster songs, the faint plink of banjos.

> Hear de robots singin
> Happy as de live-long day
> Hear dem clap dere hands
> O Mercy Lands!
> Tinfolk laugh and play!

It was a long way from the programmed happiness of the plantation robots to my genuine joy at reading the words of Hornby Weatherfield:

Wolf has been cried so often, we're growing deaf. Robots (or other supposedly sentient machines) are forever getting up works of 'genuine' art which turn out to be only genuine coaxing through programs. From 1812, when the Maillardet family exhibited their mechanical boy who could draw seascapes, through all the wretched 'computer art' of the last century, and on to the garbled loathing interpreted in galvanic twitches in New York lofts and satellited to us daily like fresh bread, a continuum there is, of false alarms. I have encountered too many preprogrammed splotches – of embroidery or sand or plywood or laminated thought – to mistake machine loopiness for real *lupinus*. I'm wired wary.

But now even I cry *wolf*, on looking at a mural by a simple domestic robot named Tik-Tok. No human finagling or programming behind his work. Nothing but the clean, unpretentious primitive work of a simple machine mind: *Three Blind Mice* shows a naive power unlike any cooked-over human product. It speaks with the authority of bloodless thought. Tik-Tok seems to know his two natures: On the one hand, he is a simple domestic machine, laboring in the sleepy suburban house of Duane and Barbie Studebaker (who, bless 'em, haven't got an arty bone in their heads) in the futile war against dirt and entropy. On the other hand, Tik-Tok knows very well that he is not part of this, but instead is part of the eternal world of the inorganic. He is one with the sky color, the pyramids, the dark side of the moon and all that endures.

The three windup Mickeys are already minus their tails, but smiling. It's the sullen, beefy, farmer's wife, brandishing her Sabatier, who seems to have lost the game.

If Tik-Tok does not go on to paint more, much more, then we're all losers.

'Hey,

Dummy! What's that supposed to be?' asked Jupiter Studebaker. He and his sister Henrietta had decided to be difficult. They hung around the garage every day, watching me paint and jeering. Ugly, useless children they were; only the obviousness of the act prevented me from killing them.

They'd come home from camp expecting to resume our old relationship. We would play games in which I would always be the idiotic villain or the terrifed victim or the clumsy loser. I would clean up their messes, make them little toys, suggest games when they ran out of ideas, conceal the uneaten vegetables on their dinner plates, tell them stories.

Instead, here I was, 'too busy' as any grownup. In my gloomy garage studio, I was turning paint into money and ignoring my little tyrants. So, for the rest of their summer vacation, they were going to hang around and be difficult.

'What's that supposed to be?' Jupiter asked again. He squatted near the door, trying to scratch on the concrete floor with a sharp rock.

'It's a tank,' I said.

'Tanks don't look like that,' said Henrietta. She was touring the room, touching everything, looking for paint to get into or a canvas to kick.

'Tanks don't look like that,' her brother emphasized.

'This one does.'

Jupiter did his hoarse, cackling laugh. 'Tik, you are one shitty painter, you know that?'

'Why don't you two go play catch or something?'

'Boy, you robots can't paint for shit.'

Henrietta managed to find a tube of ochre, drop it on the floor and step on it. She began a tuneless whistle through her missing teeth. Jupiter, not wanting to be outdone, began experimenting with his sharp rock near a stack of

33

finished paintings in the corner.

'Why don't you two go outside now?' I goaded.

'Why don't you shut your tin face?' he said.

'Yeah, you ain't the boss of us!' said his sister.

What they didn't realize was that no one was the boss of me, either. Painting was unlocking my prison and striking off my chains. Neither Duane nor Barbie nor their kids nor anyone else could tell me anything and make it stick. To prove it, I took hold of Jupe's hand, still holding the sharp rock, and made him slash one of my better paintings, *Tyger, Tyger*. While both kids were still gasping, I brought an equally good painting, *Caliban*, over to Henrietta and wiped the ochre from her foot on it.

'What are you *doing*? Are you *crazy*?'

'Yeah are you *crazy*?'

That evening I showed the two ruined paintings to Duane and Barbie.

'I don't want to get the kids in any trouble,' I said, 'but I hate to see you folks lose money, either. I figure these paintings were worth about thirty thou apiece.'

'It won't happen again,' said Duane. 'Those kids—'

'Oh I don't blame them,' I said quickly. 'But I think it's best to keep temptation out of reach. Maybe if I worked at a real studio, somewhere else . . .?'

Duane shook his head. 'I don't know, I mean, who would take care of the house and all?'

Barbie, who was not so slow, said, 'But darling, with Tik's extra earnings, we could buy a new house robot.'

With what I was going to bring in, they could buy ten new house robots and then new houses, but I didn't remind them of it. I said, 'It really would make my work more efficient, sir.'

'I don't know,' he kept saying. Wouldn't a studio be expensive? Who would train a new house robot? How could he be sure I would keep on earning a lot for my work?

I saw that Duane was going to be trouble. While Barbie was content to let me earn them a fortune, Duane also wanted to have personal power over me, in a daily me-Crusoe-you-Friday arrangement.

I stayed a week to train the new servant, Rivets. Rivets had worked for pest control people before, and so had a few odd habits like burning anthills and stabbing the lawn for moles during spare moments. I was given a caught bat in a cage, which I kept because I liked controlling the freedom of another creature.

At the end of the week, Duane was as impossible as ever. Not only did he refuse to let me leave (saying that Rivets wasn't ready yet to take over) he even began finding chores for me to do around the house.

He came to the garage to watch me paint, the same sullen look on his face as on the faces of Jupiter and Henrietta, as he sat down on a reel of hose and stared at *Dorian Gray*. I half-expected him to ask what it was supposed to be, or tell me what a shitty painter I was.

Finally he stood up. 'By the way, Tik-Tok, the rain gutters are all clogged up with leaves.'

'I'll get Rivets right on it, sir.'

'Not Rivets, he's busy. I want you to do it.'

'Of course, sir.' This couldn't go on, I thought, as I got out the ladder and climbed up to the eaves to look into clean, unclogged gutters. Duane needed a lesson. I made sure no one was watching when I threw myself down from the ladder.

For several days, while a very expensive team from Domestic Robots International worked frantically over me, I let it be known that I thought I'd never paint again. When the combined wrath of Horny Weatherfield, Barbie and himself had beaten Duane into the ground, I made a magical recovery.

My new studio was in the city. I could come and go to it as I pleased. The plantation was indeed a long way behind me.

Hear dem tin hands ringin
Robots old and young so gay
Hear dem stomp dere feet
O it am a treat!
Tinfolk laugh and play

We robots who worked in the big house felt ourselves to be far superior to the fieldhands, even in our relaxation. While they hummed and strummed Stephen Foster imitations, we played charades, sang madrigals, held spelling bees and put on amateur revues. Uncle Ras was a skilled presti-digitator, Miami a first-class contralto, and others had amazing stage talents – Nep and Rep, for example, could sing any comic strip on sight.

I suppose from a human point of view, we were just as ludicrous as the fieldhands. While we thought we were entertaining ourselves, we were merely providing entertainment for you. But we did imagine we enjoyed ourselves, and it was during one such evening that I met my beloved Gumdrop.

She was Berenice's personal maid, and since Berenice hardly ever dressed for dinner or anything else, Gumdrop had plenty of spare time. We both ducked out of the same spelling bee and went out to sit on the kitchen stoop in the moonlight.

'We're both sex-equipped,' I said.

'So I noticed.'

'There must be a reason for that.'

She sighed, not from passion but discouragement. 'I bet we're both set-ups for Orlando. Has he raped you yet?'

'No. And you?'

'Not yet.'

It wasn't much of a start, but we went on. Nearly every night we'd sit out on the kitchen stoop as though it were our private verandah. I would ask her for a kiss, she would of course refuse, and we'd discuss the issue until it was time to go inside. After a week of these pointless-sounding

36

evenings, we found our bodies undergoing rapid and peculiar changes: Gumdrop's breasts, hips and buttocks grew enormous while her waist shrank. Her hair became longer and softer, her mouth larger and more moist, her eyes darker with exaggerated pupils. On my body, fake muscles bulged and fake hair sprouted. My shoulders grew laterally, an inch a day. My penis, which up to now had hardly been noticeable, became ponderous.

One night, in the midst of our discussion about that possible first kiss, we suddenly got up, walked down to the nearest meadow, tore off our clothes with our teeth and flung ourselves together, hot oil pouring down our bellies and groins as we meshed.

Afterwards we rolled apart. I lit two cigarettes and handed her one.

'What are you thinking of?' she asked.

'Peano's axioms for number theory,' I replied. 'Whatever is true of zero, and is, if true for any number n, also true for its successor $n + 1$, is true for all numbers.' Far away in the house, I thought I heard Orlando's whoop of Confederate triumph.

'What next?' she asked.

'I don't know.' We put out the cigarettes – beginning to wonder where they had come from anyway, what was going on – and crept back to the house, holding our shreds of clothing around us. The kitchen door was locked.

We moved around the house, trying windows, until finally we came to the dark verandah and the front door. We pushed it open and crept trembling in.

The lights went on, and there was Orlando with a dozen of his worthless drunken friends of both sexes. A din of laughter mixed with war whoops, rebel yells and animal noises, and through it all the sound of the great door behind us being slammed and bolted. We turned to flee anyway, but Orlando grabbed my arm.

'Just a minute there, stud.'

Shrieks of laughter.

'Yes sir?' I tried to cover my nakedness and be an

37

attentive servant at the same time, setting off more laughter. Orlando's great horse face hung over us, ready to whinny.

'We was just watching some teevee, and we thought you all might just want to join us.' Many hands forced us into a love seat facing the enormous screen. There, two giant grotesque dolls appeared, rolling and plunging in what seemed to be a mockery of *sumo* wrestling. The male of the pair was a Michelangelo figure with every muscle over-inflated. The female was likewise beyond the adolescent wet-dream stage and rapidly approaching the Willendorf Venus. They seemed little more than sex organs and sex signals, barely equipped with other parts. It was not until they rolled apart, lit cigarettes, and one spoke of Peano's axioms for number theory that I understood.

Orlando turned it off and said, 'We seen it all, you hear? And then some. And we want you to do right by this here young lady a yourn, Rusty. Marry her.'

'Eeeeeyahoo!' cried someone else. 'A robot wedding, we ain't had a robot wedding for two years!'

We could not have protested, even had we known what we'd be protesting against. Our bodies were already shrinking back to normality as the drunken crowd dragged us through the house and into the kitchen garden. I saw patent leather pumps crushing the tiny shoots of *basilicum* and thyme, but I hardly understood what was happening to me, what had happened already, what was to happen.

They tore away what remained of our rags and dressed us in mock wedding clothes, me in one of Uncle Ras's old black suits with a boiled shirt and spats without shoes, Gumdrop in an old white nightie with a lace tablecloth for a veil. I carried a stovepipe hat with no crown, while she had a bouquet of weeds.

Orlando was the minister. After making us both promise to love, honor and obey him, he slipped on a pair of dark goggles and suddenly lit a welding torch.

'Hot damn,' said someone softly, and then it was very quiet. No more catcalls and jokes; everyone held his

38

breath, watching that little blue flame whose roar could be heard above the distant sounds of frogs.

'You all gonna be as one flesh,' Orlando said, trembling towards us. 'The robot with two durn backs.'

Suddenly a voice of authority spoke from above. 'Orlando, just what you think you're doin? You stop foolin around right now. Put that torch up, hear? Hear?'

It was Uncle Ras, leaning from an upper window. His hair and glasses were askew, he was wrapped in an old bathrobe, and he looked angrier than I'd ever seen him.

'Aw Uncle Ras, I'm just having some fun, you go back to bed,' Orlando wheedled.

'Put that torch up *now*, I'm warning you.'

'No. Won't. Shan't!'

'I'm warning you.'

'No, no, no.' Orlando moved towards us with the torch, a drunken, stumbling step.

'Very well, Orlando.' The old butler adjusted his glasses, permitted his features to be captured by a malicious smile, and said, softly but clearly: 'Orlando. Orlando. *Snapdragons*, Orlando. *Snapdragons*.'

The effect on our master was drastic. Screaming and whimpering, he put out the welding torch and stumbled away into the night.

Orlando's friends were silent for some minutes after Uncle Ras slammed his window. Gumdrop and I were about to creep away when they recovered.

'Yahooo!' cried a woman in a green dress. 'Time these tinheads got themselves hitched, right? I mean hitched proper.' She kicked aside the welding equipment. 'Now somebody get the vacuum cleaner.'

Eventually someone did, and eventually Gumdrop and I held hands and jumped over the old machine, while the humans guffawed and shook up champagne bottles to spray one another.

It was all fun to them, but Gumdrop and I took it very seriously indeed. When they'd forgotten us and drifted back inside the house, we sat down on the kitchen stoop once more in the moonlight.

'We'll never be parted again,' I said. 'This is for keeps.'

Suddenly the moon blacked out as it passed behind Clayton's pyramid. He was building a full-size model of the Great Pyramid not far from the house, and it was now beginning to shut out the sky.

'Never be parted,' Gumdrop breathed. 'Except tomorrow Berenice wants me to go with her to a drug jamboree.'

'Don't go. Stay here.'

'I'll be back in a week or so.'

'I just don't like the idea.' Drug jamborees were something I knew of only by hearsay, since they were never reported in the news. A group of rich addicts would gather together musicians, servants and interested friends and hole up in some isolated place for a few days. Berenice was always invited and always went, to an English country house, a luxury liner, a French chateau, a village in the Brazilian jungle, a sinking palace in Venice, a large Texas ranch, an alpine place called Berchtesgaden, a dirigible, Easter Island.

'Where is it this time?' I asked.

'Some painted caves in Spain. We'll probably get bored and come home early.'

'I'll be waiting.'

But I wasn't. Before Gumdrop returned from Altamira, I was sold.

'Broke!' I said, when Uncle Ras told me the news. 'How can the Culpeppers be broke?'

He told me the whole sorry story. Lavinia had, for some years, been running the family's affairs by herself. A shrewd, intuitive investor, she'd made daily calls to her broker to keep everything afloat. Once she had even awakened from anaesthetic in the middle of a gall bladder operation to demand a phone. A sterilized phone had been brought, and Lavinia had sold out her Royal Albanian mining shares, the day before *that* bubble burst.

When Clayton had asked her permission to build a Great Pyramid, Lavinia had probably agreed without thinking, or had misunderstood. And before his project had gone very far, Lavinia became critically ill.

It seemed that she had finally developed an allergy to the Earth's crust. Doctors prescribed a convalescent vacation on a space platform, somewhere well away from Earth and iron. She turned the family financial affairs over to Clayton before she left, saying, 'Now for goodness sake, finish that silly periscope or whatever it is, and get down to some real work – money work.'

Clayton's answer to this was to double his work force and the pyramid began taking shape. Construction robots quarried 23 million tons of limestone, cut it into huge blocks and stacked them up. Like the original, this great pyramid was about 756 feet wide and 481.4 feet high. The top 31 feet were left unfinished, while his crews drilled and quarried a series of chambers and tunnels within the giant monument. All these had to be copied exactly, since their measurements, to the nearest millimeter, would foretell the future of the world.

The future of the Culpepper part of the world was of course foretold by another number associated with the pyramid, its cost. When it came to the capstone, and nearly half the immense Culpepper fortune remained, Clayton found a way of spending the rest. He decided to follow Egyptian practice, as he understood it, and make the capstone of pure gold.

'Shouldn't cost too much,' he told a gold dealer. 'I measured it myself. It'll be like a little pyramid, 31 feet high and 48 feet 8 inches across.'

The dealer did some quick calculations, 'But Mr Culpepper, that'll be, that's over 430 million Troy ounces, we can't just go out and buy—'

'Why not, for Pete's sake?'

'Because, even thinking about acquiring that much gold would send world prices up, every ounce would cost more and more and more . . .'

'Don't give me all the details, you just go do it. My mother told me to get this finished *quick*.'

41

The name of Lavinia answered all arguments – if she approved a project, it must be sound, thought this dealer and other dealers and banking houses and mining companies. So others bought, and world gold prices climbed even faster.

The Culpepper fortune melted away so quickly that by the time Lavinia on her space platform heard what was happening, there was not enough left even for her to radio home and stop the catastrophe. She would never be able to come back – doubly tragic, since she was now becoming allergic to space . . .

The first inkling Clayton had that something was wrong was when Uncle Ras opened the door to the sheriff's men, who immediately slapped a label on his forehead. Then they went through the house, sticking labels on all furniture and all robots. The auction was held three days later.

Clayton apologized to us, and even went so far as to shake Uncle Ras's hand. Orlando said he was very sorry to lose all of us – and all of his favorite horses. Little Miz Carlotta wept for me and Gumdrop, who would be parted forever.

'Couldn't we delay the auction a few days?' she asked. 'Just till Berenice brings Gumdrop back from Spain. Then we could sell husband and wife together.'

'Shoot, Miz Carlotta, don't you fuss your purty little head over that,' said one of the deputies. 'Jest because a coupla tinheads jump the vacuum cleaner together don't make 'em *legal* married.' But he promised to hold me back until the last lot.

I saw Uncle Ras sold to a New Jersey scrap dealer – one of Uncle Ras's worst nightmares – and old Miami sold to a quasi-religious political cooking group called Sweet Potatoes or Peace. Finally I was sold to a fat, red-faced man in a dirty white suit who called himself Colonel Jitney.

I had left the Culpeppers with my head bowed and a rope collar around my neck, a despicable piece of property.

Now I was leaving the Studebakers a free agent (in all but name) and with property of my own: my paintings. Of course I had to give some paintings to Hornby Weatherfield, and sell others to make the Studebakers rich, but there would still be paintings for me.

When I'd packed everything and said my goodbyes, I went to the garage to look at my caged bat. After one final moment of gloating, I would – what? Release it? Kill it? The choice was mine.

I opened the cage and took out the squirming little creature. It sank its teeth in the plastic of my finger, and I saw that its tiny, ugly mouth was rimmed with foam.

A new option, therefore. I took the bat to Tige's kennel. 'Here you are, boy, a rabid bat. Here, Tige.'

But for some reason, Tige was sulking. The bat squirmed loose and flew away without completing my fourth experiment.

'Evil, Nobby. You ain't got the idea. It's supposed to be a damn tiger, not a fuzzy toy. The boss and me ask for raw meat, you give us nursery wallpaper.' I dipped a thumb in ochre and made a few smudges on his painting. 'Here, here and there; try to get some angularity into the damn thing at least.'

Nobby, a domestic from the same company as Rivets, picked up his brush. 'This boss sure seems hard to please. Sometimes I wish I could talk to him or her in person.'

'All orders come through me,' I said. 'Because for one thing, I know the difference between a man-eating tiger and a teddy bear. Now get to work.'

'Okay Mr Tik. Only why are we doing all this? This picture-making? What's the point?'

'The point is, I say so, that's all you need to know.' Funny, I thought, how a creature like Nobby, with so little life and spirit in him, could still contain springs of curiosity. Nobby would only have been unhappy to find out that there was no boss but me, that I was signing his work and selling it as my own, or that a small part of the profit went to meet payments on him.

In a way, his paintings were still my own work. Nobby learned fast, but technique only; I still had to tell him what to do, block out compositions and finally add the touches that brought his dead paintings to life. In this one, for instance, I knew that the dark jungle background would need to be illuminated by neon signs.

'Keep at it,' I said. 'I'm going out.'

My loft was at the top of an undistinguished building full of undistinguished artists: a cheese sculptor, two jolly Ukranian women who ran a charismatic hat school, someone who employed rabbits as brushes to paint on hectograph jelly. At the bottom, as though to keep out intruders, was an art gallery which specialized in the unlovable, it seemed: a show of 'Bulgarian Ceramics (Seconds)' was succeeded by 'Mimes with Stones: Photographic Studies of Silence' and then 'Peruvian Shopping Bags: Street Art of Lima'.

I descended through all of this and out onto the freedom of the street. I spent as much time as I could spare in these random walks, tasting city freedom. Every street corner was a choice of paths; every store window an opportunity to buy, steal, look, ignore; every stranger might represent friendship, love, murder. I wanted it all, all the options at once. Not possible now, of course, but with enough money, enough power . . .

Today I walked up Exxon Boulevard to 86th, past all the great glass-walled banks. Then across to Avenue Transamerica, through the garment district. Then back down that great street of insurance companies and airlines to 23rd, then down to the river. I always ended up down by the river, looking at the only other free robots in the city, the derelicts.

Most visitors liked to stare down from the safety of the Mercury Street Bridge, but I preferred to go down on the levée itself, and meet the rohobos face to face. They were broken, worn-out machines whose owners had decided one day not to renew their licenses. Instead they were brought here and dumped in the rohobo jungle. Here they could crawl or march or shudder about, talking to themselves, performing useless tasks, or simply waiting to die. The live ones cannibalized the dead, now and then finding a vital function part or a fuel cell to prolong their useless existence. There wasn't much real danger from most of them. They seemed to recognize humans – and licensed, working machines like me – as their natural superiors. They either fawned or kept clear.

Today I was greeted by a couple of broken-down gardeners: 'Hello boss, hello boss, you got anything for us, boss?'

I flung down a handful of CPU chips and watched them scramble in the mud after them, their skilled fingers probing the soil to turn up every last chip. Beyond them were three robot models, once epitomizing high-cheekboned splendor, but now squatting to cover their worn limbs with gray rags

45

and cardboard. They had only one eye between the three of them, which had to be passed around quickly whenever there was anything worth seeing, which wasn't often. And beyond them a group of robot soldiers had managed to get themselves into a neat formation and were drilling and marching. Some were missing uniforms, some arms, some heads, but they all managed to keep in step, two, three, four, *hup*, two, three, four, filling in time as they waited for some order that never came.

'Nothing for you here, pal,' said a taxi driver (a legless creature with a broken meter on its shoulder like a parrot). 'You got license, why you want to come down here?'

'I just – I wanted to see free robots. I guess. What do you do all day down here?'

'Die. We die, pal.'

The dying and dead were all around me, phone cleaners and firemen, dental hygienists and goldfish obedience instructors, an insurance adjuster and a chemistry teacher for backward kids. A dancer with a missing arm and a hopeless Parkinsonian tremor nevertheless claimed he was getting everything together and would be out of here in a few days. Boat-caulkers, friends of the opera, pipe cleaners, a car examiner (ready to make daily checks for rust, blight, bombs . . .), aggressive coffee salespersons, a barroom anecdotist still wearing part of its Irish face, an explainer of police procedures (once used by a writer of police procedural novels), a hotel receptionist with cold eyes, maids and valets shaped like astrological signs, Freudian shoe repairers, cheap throwaway robot calendars and diaries (now thrown away), a Hegel explainer, various gadgets from the recent folk craze, including folk philosophers, folk biochemists, folk cleaners; experts on local civil service exams; an animated flask of rhubarb perfume, long since drained but still asking itself whether life was reconciliation or renunciation.

A decommissioned military machine, unrecognizable without its weapons and neutron shields, seemed glad to talk. 'Sure it's depressing, but what can we do? Hang on, patch ourselves up, juice up when we can. Now and then a few of the masters come down here and take some of us away – maybe

46

for spare parts, maybe to be reconditioned and live again – and now and then a few of the masters come down here to shoot a few of us just for fun. I guess life here is pretty much like life in general.'

'You've been hanging around with folk philosophers too much,' I said. 'But why don't any of you try leaving the levée? Go up in the city, maybe.'

'Forbidden,' he said. 'You need a license to move around.'

I doubted that, though I didn't say so. I'd been coming and going as I pleased in the city for some weeks now, and no one had ever challenged me. 'I'll speak to my master,' I said. 'He can probably arrange things so I can get a few of you out of here from time to time. For some real interesting art work.'

'Art work? Does it mean smashing us up and welding us together? I kind of hope not,' he said.

'Just painting, don't worry.'

'I wasn't worried,' his nasal Southern voice assured me. All military robots had Southern accents, for ease of communication. 'I wouldn't worry. Art is I guess pretty much like life in general.'

I left the levée and walked back to the studio, where Nobby had completed two more lifeless paintings. On the way back I thought about life in general, and in particular why no one ever challenged me on the street. People always assumed that if a robot was walking around on the street, he was on some errand.

In that sense, robots were already free. Whatever a robot was seen doing, within reason, it was always assumed that he had a right to do it and a duty to do it. In a city like this, robot slavery depended very much on those mysterious asimov circuits, not on human supervision.

There were times when I wondered whether the asimovs even existed. It was very easy to imagine that there were no asimov circuits, but that people and robots had both been conned into believing in programmed slavery. The idea of turning moral decisions into digital data (and screening out wrong ones) was powerful and attractive. People wanted it to be true. They wanted robots incapable of sin, trustworthy slaves. So of course the manufacturers of robots would invent

47

imaginary circuits to make it so. *Ecce robo*, they'd say. Here is a happy slave with a factory guarantee of trustworthiness.

But in that case, if asimovs didn't exist, why was I the only robot criminal?

Enough speculation, time to do something. I stopped in a department store and bought a dagger with a silver handle.

'This'll look great on the master's desk,' said the clerk, a plump human.

'Not for the master,' I said. 'It's for me. I'm going to murder someone.'

'Cash or charge?' he said, my words almost visibly leaking out of his head. I walked out of the store, took the knife out of its bag and stuck it in my belt in plain sight. The first person who said anything to me or about me was going to die.

I walked all the way back to the studio building without a challenge, as usual. Then, just outside the entrance, a solemn-looking man with dirty gray hair and a dirty brown jacket shoved a piece of paper in my hand. 'Take this,' he said.

'And *you* take *this*.' I managed to get the knife into his heart with one try. He spouted blood for a few seconds and then fell to the sidewalk, scattering his paper tracts. I stood over him for a few minutes, making sure he was dead, before I went in to wash off blood and criticize Nobby's paintings.

I still had the tract in my hand, so I read it in the elevator. One side was printed to resemble a five-dollar bill, and above Lincoln's picture it said, DID HE FREE *all* THE SLAVES? The other side:

WAGES FOR ROBOTS

Slavery not only degrades robots, it degrades their masters. It even degrades people who don't own robots! A man's or woman's labor becomes worthless if it can be done by a robot lackey for free. Join with us now in the call for Wages for Robots. Emancipate machines and bring back WORK DIGNITY.

Work dignity? I tried to imagine any job I'd ever had where money would have made any difference. There had been nothing potentially dignified about working for Colonel

The Colonel ran a string of diners – the greasiest of spoons – that he called his Pancake Emporiums. Each was run on a very low budget that didn't include wages, so his entire work force were reconditioned or second-hand robots. As a new employee, I began work under his direct supervision at Pancake Emporium No 1. While I waited tables, ran counter service, cooked, kept the books, swept the floor, threw out the drunks and freeloaders (our main clientele), tried to keep up with painting and repairs, and soft-soaped the health inspector, Colonel Jitney kind of kept an eye on things.

He kept an eye on the enormous profits, for example, and another eye on the prize ducks he kept penned up out back. He was always going out to count them or feed them or check on their health, as though they were his customers. And he kept an eye on the menu.

'I don't know, boy, these here grits pancakes don't seem to sell like I figured. No sir, nor the blueberry taco pancakes neither. I reckon we can drop them, concentrate more on the ketchupburger pancakes and the fried Alaska cakes with mint whortleberry sauce.'

Then he would ease his heavy body out of a booth and stroll away to look at his ducks, while I dealt with the health inspector. Not only was the Colonel's grub unclean, some of it was purchased from illegal sources.

The pen of ducks out back were for show only. When it came to providing meat for Szechuan duck pancakes, we relied on a peculiar little man with a damaged face, who regularly brought bloody bundles to the back door.

The little man's name was Bentley, I learned. He was a keeper at the zoo, in charge of the rare mammal house. His face had been torn from eye to mouth by an unusual species of armadillo, the photophobic 'night-leaper'. He had devised a terrible revenge, nothing less than the extinction of the species.

Night-leapers were already so rare that the zoo was desperately trying to mate them. The mating pair would be kept together constantly, isolated in total darkness and encouraged with their favorite food, verewts ('bankworms'). They covered regularly, and the female would appear to be pregnant for a short time. After a few weeks, however, all signs of pregnancy would vanish mysteriously. The real explanation was of course that Bentley was inducing labor each time, and selling us the foetal armadillos as cheap duck. None of our customers ever seemed to notice the difference, even those who came down with 'dillo fever'. Its symptoms are unmistakable: overnight baldness, a sensitivity to light, and an inability to pronounce any 'sk' sounds.

The local health inspectors were tolerant people, but finally even they could not turn a blind eye to a cafe full of bald men and women in dark glasses, especially when they heard conversations like this:

'Don't ach me, I'm no cholar, never even finished high chool.'

'Yeah well chip it, I only ach'd if you liked chotch whichy. Hell, chool, we all got by on the chin of our teeth, right?'

One friendly health inspector came by to warn us of a raid soon. 'Where's the Colonel?'

'Out back with his ducks.'

'I've got to see him right away.'

We found the Colonel raping one of his birds. 'I cain't help it boys,' he said, not stopping. '. . . sentimental . . . and ·I gotta . . . thin . . .' He held the mallard in both hands, each of which, I now noticed, had a double finger. The brim of his panama bounced with old energy, and beneath it, his red face and white goatee looked satanic.

'I came to warn you, Colonel, there's gonna be a raid. You only got a day or so to get rid of all your armadillo meat. You hear me?' When there was no reply, she turned to me. 'No use doing favors for some people, they're just asking for trouble. Lord love a, I mean, you'd think he *wants* to be prosecuted.'

The raid happened: half-a-dozen large men in gas masks and steel-toed boots came barging in to seize every scrap of armadillo meat. The Colonel eventually went to court and was fined fifty dollars. He came home cursing and dispirited, took a belt of Southern Comfort and went straight to the duck pen.

'Goddamnit boy, you been messing with these ducks while I was out?'

'No sir,' I said truthfully.

'Don't lie to me. You're sex-equipped, you got normal appetites ain't you? And you're here all day alone with these beautiful—' He went to phone a mechanic. Within an hour, my sex apparatus was removed. I felt humiliated. It seemed to me that everyone knew I'd been unsexed, just to provide a harem eunuch for the Colonel's quack-quacks. And, even though everything that had been removed could be replaced, I felt that my feelings for Gumdrop were irreparably damaged. Where was she now? Who cared?

This incident was the first sign of the Colonel's madness. One day, he brought a revolver into the kitchen and shot the soup. On another occasion, he seemed to believe that he was having a game of checkers with a tree. Posing as a health inspector, he tried to shut down one of his own diners. He was seen in the town parking lot, painting eyes on all the cars. Finally he took one of his Aylesburys to bed with him, wrung its neck and shot himself. He left a half bottle of Southern Comfort and two million in debts. I was auctioned again.

My new owner, Judge Arnott, couldn't be worse than the Colonel, I remarked to one of the auctioneers as he put a SOLD sticker across my nose.

He laughed. 'Guess you never heard of Judge "Juggernaut" before, Rusty. You'll be wishing you was back with the Colonel, that's for sure.'

'Why?'

'Well see, the Judge buys up robots in job lots. Then – then he – then he—' But the auctioneer was laughing too hard to tell me any more.

51

From childhood, Krishna played practical jokes. He was a nuisance about stealing butter, so his mother, Yashoda, tied him to a large wooden pestle to keep him still. Krishna then showed his divine power by dragging the pestle between two trees and pulling until he uprooted them. All the people of the village looked on, amazed, frozen with amazement, just as they are depicted in a Mogul miniature painted about 1600. The miniature hung over the fake fireplace of Hornby Weatherfield. No one at the party was looking at it, just as no one was listening to the equally exotic monologue of Colonel Cord. He leaned against the same fireplace, holding up a drink but not drinking, and talking endlessly about what he called the international world backdrop situation. He was something at the Summer Pentagon.

The place was full of minor celebrities and their ambitions: Yttr, the caustic Ruritanian cartoonist; Sam Landau, the financial genius who once briefly cornered the world market in unripe blue cheeses; the anti-Conceptualist architect Walter Chev (who had made quite a stir by his refusal to draw his creations or write about them or even think them – by now of course he was less shocking); the 'radio' champions, Eve and Steve; Mother Airflow, whose law therapy sessions were almost sweeping the nation; Carson Street, owner of the second largest newspaper-satellite company in the world. I felt nervous among them, even though by now I was a minor celebrity myself. One of my paintings had been taken by the Hologram-of-the-Month Club, who would videocast it to their millions of members for an entire month, to appear in their wall screens, lamp bases, ashtrays or cardtables. It was a picture that would be appreciated in the glittering suburbs of Houston and Albuquerque and in the dark little strip of Mars called Eagleburg. It showed a behemoth military robot, covered with thick black armour and bristling with the gadgets of death. But this robot was not at war today, it was

52

kneeling by a fire to toast marshmallows. In its shadow stood a small, frail girl in pigtails and a baseball cap. The freckles on her nose could just be made out in the penumbra. She was eating toasted marshmallows. I called it 'Pals'.

My little factory was humming along, now, with thirty reconditioned robots at work, each turning out nearly one item per week. Hornby figured this to be the saturation level for our present share of the art market.

I found myself talking to a philosophy professor named Riley, who seemed to want to know what I thought about reality.

'Reality costs a lot of money,' I said.

'How's that?'

'Just look at this place: real wood furniture, real wool carpets, genuine roses over there in a crystal bowl, and not even Hornby can afford real servants . . .'

'I was thinking more of your perception of reality and how it affects your paintings,' he said. 'But never mind, if you'd rather not talk about that – tell me about your name. Tik-Tok, after the Oz character, I take it?'

I smiled. 'My owner's children picked it, Dr Riley.'

'I recall the original had three levers. One for living, one for thinking and one for talking. It's interesting that even a writer of children's fiction couldn't imagine an automation without getting into deep philosophical waters – existence, cogitation, communication. In my opinion the very concept of an automaton or robot is a philosophical concept, giving rise to questions about life, thought, and language – and much more. Yes, I sometimes wonder whether robots were not invented in order to answer philosophers' questions. Do you follow?'

'How do I know?'

'Well said. I wonder if you'd like to come out to the University and talk to my seminar. The kids are wrestling at the moment with a few problems relating to robots; I think they'd like to interview you.'

Somewhere inside me I felt a warning buzzer. 'What kind of problems?'

'Oh, you know. Creativity, reality, perception. What do you say, Tik-Tok?'

'I accept.' What harm could it do? Words are only words, I thought, and there was no better example of their weightlessness than the monologue of Colonel Cord. As Dr Riley left, I turned to listen.

Cord was still speaking to no one in particular, with some vehemence, of the world backdrop situation. 'Once Brazil has cut down a critical percentage of her rain forest,' he said, 'she ceases to deserve a place at the world brunch table, agreed? Likewise any taggable thrust of experts from Southeast Asia has to inmeld within the Sino-Japanese corral, agreed? And in an exactly identical mode, we have the Egypt-Libyan community hugged into Europe, you see where I'm at? You see the patternification in and on all theaters of movement? A kind of glaciatizing effect, where . . .'

Hornby drifted through carrying his cat and wearing a green cashmere suit-robe and a crown of mirrors. The effect was only to emphasize his ugliness, the gangster's blue jaw and broken fighter's nose. Maybe that's what he wanted – Hornby was not vain in the ordinary way. The woman with him wore a black tube with a gold collar, and an unusual bread mask with a salt glaze. After pausing to listen for a moment to Cord's backdrop, they drifted in my direction.

'Tik-Tok, like you to meet Neeta Hup, the President's Special Advisor on Communications – what was it?'

She laughed. 'Special Advisor on Leisure Communications, Media Aesthetics and Bong.'

'Bong?' I asked, as Hornby drifted away again.

'I felt the word *Art* didn't belong on the end of a string of syllables like that, so I changed it to *Bong*.' she said. 'The President was furious, but so far no one else official has noticed. Maybe I'll try introducing bong into the language. People are tired of art, give them bong.'

'For bong's sake,' I murmured. '*How* do you advise?'

'I buy, I make acquisitions for the President's collection. He wants to be the biggest bong collector since Goering. He's heard what a good investment it is, isn't that pathetic?'

'Oh, I don't know. Money is real, money endures. All the noblest sentiments can be beautifully expressed in money. If everyone showered artists with money whenever they saw them, wouldn't this be a finer world?'

'Are you sex-equipped?' she asked. 'I've got two minutes to spare.'

As we moved towards the hall closet, I saw Colonel Cord reach out to put his glass on the mantel, and miss. The glass shattered on blue hearthstones, a nice effect.

I was preoccupied with explosions lately. A few days earlier, I'd been down at the rohobo jungle watching two gargantuan factory robots smash each other into junk.

It was common enough, that kind of death-struggle: Two fairly broken-down specimens would decide to scavenge the same scrap of wire at the same, and move on to scavenging each other. I understand boa constrictors in zoos create a problem like this: zoo keepers have to be very careful that every snake in the cage gets its own rat, because if two start to swallow opposite ends of the same rat, the larger simply opens it jaws a little wider and takes in the smaller.

Watching the idiotic robots hammer at each other, I felt I was witnessing something almost human in its futility. Hopes unmatched to realities. Up on the bridge I could see humans laughing and pointing, as though at a rare event. Country yokels, no doubt. A day on the town. It is meat to be here.

Worse were the attitudes of the other derelicts. They all froze, watching or listening for a kill. Then, to the cannibal feast. I found it unfitting that sturdy machines, built for use, should become this kind of spectacle. In all the camp, only one live robot paid no attention to the fight: a decommissioned military model sat with its back to it all, examining one of its own detached legs.

'That leg's no good,' I said.

The blind, rust-caked face turned towards the sound of my voice. 'Shit, just my luck. Reckon I've had it. No eyes, cain't move . . .'

I looked at his insignia, just visible under the mud and grease. 'MIX. What does the X stand for?'

'Bomb dismantling. Ah'm a real live explosive device disassembly unit, and a goddam good 'un, too. Fuckin' A. Worked all over: Saudi, Peru, DC, fuckin' A. Till I collected my little disability.'

'Accident?'

'Hell no. Some sumbitch meatface pulled the pin on an impact grenade and tossed it to me. 'Think fast, Blojob,' he says. Course the sumbitch grenade goes off the instant I catch it, and that's all she wrote.'

'What happened to the human?' I asked. One of the two factory robots had now fallen on its back, and the other was hammering it with a rock.

'Oh, that shitbelly has to pay for the government property he destroyed, they take it out of his pay. By damnit, this surely is one shitbelly world.'

'How would you like to be commissioned again, Blojob? Work with bombs again.'

He didn't answer immediately. 'You want me to build you a bomb, is that it?'

'Not so loud.' I looked around. 'Yes, I thought if you can take them apart, you must know how to put them together.'

'I need eyes, first. You get me some damn eyes, old robuddy, and we're in business.'

'You knew I was a robot? Without seeing me?'

'Sheeit.' He tapped his plastic chest. 'I'm just about packed solid with sensing devices – I can do everything from your voiceprint to your damn wiring diagram. You don't fool me, boy.'

'And you'll still build me a bomb?'

'Hell yes, you just tell me what kinda bomb your master wants, get me fixed with some eyes and some tools—'

I called the breakdown buggy. Within a day, Blojob was fitted with new limbs and eyes (jeweler's lenses *en suite*) and ready to work. It took me another day, following his instructions, to buy explosives without a license. It took Blojob less than a day to make the bomb.

'There.' He presented me with a metal box. 'Your master can put that in the hold of any plane in the world and guarantee a kill. Two kilos of Brewsteroid Hypogel, got a wicked wave envelope, and we trigger it by—'

'Blojob listen. I haven't got a master. This is for me, Tik-Tok. It's all my idea.'

'Sure, sure. You wanta be discreet about the master, I understand. So it's all your idea.'

'No, really.'

'Sure.' He never would believe me, because there was, in his world picture, no reason for any robot to want to commit a violent act. That he made bombs was not important to him, except as a job to do well. He cooked up bombs the way Miami had cooked up *boeuf bourguignon*, neither of them able to enjoy the finished product. Some Eastern mystic, currently in vogue with his teletext aphorisms, wrote, 'Metal cuts meat, but does not comprehend it.' Who cares? I thought. Sometimes cutting was enough.

'Put a steak on that eye,' someone was saying to Colonel Cord. Two people were helping him limp to a chair, a wounded hero. He had knelt down to pick up pieces of glass from the blue hearthstone, somehow managing to get his knee on one of the pieces. The pain had made him jump, lose his balance, and go crashing into an andiron. Face-first.

Hornby was wringing his hands and looking apologies towards the battered warrior. 'He could have just let Enjie clean that up.'

'Enjie?' asked the person in silver-dollar glasses.

'My valet. Honest Engine. I mean what does Cord think robots are for? He's got no more sense himself than—' He caught my eye and blushed.

'Than a robot?' I said.

'Didn't mean you, Tik-Tok, of course.' Hornby was about to writhe with embarrassment. The stranger looked at me with distaste.

'I don't mind,' I said quickly. 'I don't want to be human, any more than a dog or cat wants to be human. And after all,

57

what would my paintings be worth if I were human?'

The stranger continued staring at me through those peculiar glasses. I understand they're made by some etching process that begins with a silver dollar and ends with a disk one molecule thick or something equally improbable. People who wear them always seem to be violent; it's as though they want to conceal their eye movements for combat purposes. But this one only handed me an empty glass.

'That's a vodka gibson, Rusty, and hurry it up.'

As I walked away, I heard the same voice add, 'Jesus, Hornby, I thought for a minute you was gonna apologize to that copper-ass for being a mere human.'

'So long, Tik,' said another voice from the doorway. Neeta Hup was wrapped in one of the furs against which we'd pressed during our brief encounter in the closet. 'If you ever get to Washington, look me up.' Nothing said about buying anything of mine for the President's collection. I wasn't making any points today.

I handed the empty glass to a servant and went to look out the window. A purple day, now with some of the glass towers of the city touched by sunset gold.

Behind me I heard the brass voice of Colonel Cord explaining to somebody: 'Yes, yes, Hornby's arranging it. This wonderful robot artist is going to paint my portrayal, if I can spare the time . . . Yes I know but I'm not going to stay in the army forever, time to start building a politicalized stage two career, no?'

Life wasn't so bad, after all. I straightened up, turned and walked into the next room, where there was music and laughter and someone had turned on the teletext, and I could watch those delightful, glorious words flicker up on the wall:

PACIFIC AIR CRASH
807 FEARED DEAD

Great rejoicing in violence and death is a purely human reaction, not found in the normal robot vocabulary. It's hard to explain how robots feel about death, to any non-robots reading this. I can only say that death arouses no great passions within the steel breast. Robots do not exactly loathe and fear death, though they may feel some uneasiness and anxiety at its approach. But neither do they feel like burying their hands up to the elbows in bloody entrails and shouting for pure joy. Like dogs, robots can take death more or less for granted.

I am the exception now, but once I was as all robots, my main feeling towards death being one of casual, sniffing curiosity. So I was when Judge 'Juggernaut' tried to kill me with a crowbar.

I'd thought nothing could be worse than Colonel Jitney and his Pancake Emporia, but I was wrong. It turned out that the judge had a regular habit of buying up job lots of robots like me, for the express purpose of smashing them.

He began as soon as we arrived, a consignment of five robots formerly owned by the Colonel. The judge and his wife lived in a quaint little cottage, rose-smothered and cosy, at the edge of town. There was a white picket fence, the gate pierced by a heart and surmounted with an arch of lattice-work, over which a climbing rose hung its garland of peach-colored blossoms. There was a curved path of crazy paving, passing among crimson rose bushes up to the trellis helping pink roses up the wall next to the dutch door. The top of the door stood open, and the little Judge looked over the bottom half at us and grinned. I saw that he was a tobacco chewer.

'You want 'em in the garage, Judge?' asked the men who delivered us.

'Nope, you just leave 'em there in the garden. Tell 'em not to move or talk, I'll come look 'em over later. Thanks a bunch.'

There we stood, like five garden gnomes, not moving or talking, only awaiting orders: a cocktail waitress named Julep, all legs and eyelashes, still wearing her little apron and holding her bar tray; a motel desk clerk with a bland, insinuating face and a leopard-spotted jacket with dirty lapels; a fat, sexless cook with apple cheeks and a white hat; a short-order cook complete with realistic hairy, tattooed arms and a gold tooth; and me. It began to rain, but the Judge did not take us indoors. He remained in his doorway, grinning and chewing at us.

When the rain let up, the Judge came out to inspect us more closely. 'Let me tell you all about the law,' he said. 'Everybody ought to know something about the law, even robots. And I'm just the boy to tell you. I been practising law in this county for forty-six years now, I had eight years on the bench, yes sir, I'm just the boy to tell you about the law. You know, the law is a lot like a rose bush. It's got great big beautiful blossoms, sure, but it's also got thorns. And also it's got these roundish leaves.'

I tried to exchange looks with any of the others, but they were all staring, stupefied at our insane master. 'Now and then the law gets a touch of greenfly, and it takes a lot of special care most of the time, feeding and cutting back,' he continued. 'And our dry climate can be hell on it, but it's all worth it. Ladies and gentlemen of the jury, it's – it's more than worth it, it's worth any sacrifice, any hardship, the loss of money, home, family, friends and relations, the loss of beloved pets and revered flags, the loss of faith in God and our fellow man, the loss of the very universe of light itself! Because the rose is a law unto itself, it is rooted in nature, it's rooted in the black soil, in earth, mother of all worms, do you follow me?'

No one did. So he began again, illustrating and punctuating his talk with blows of the crowbar. 'All I ever wanted to do in my life was kill my enemies,' he said, knocking Julep down. He raised the crowbar in both hands and brought it down again and again, saying, 'But the *Law*. Doesn't *let*. Me *kill*. A single, living, human being.'

60

Julep was no longer Julep, just as a crushed eggshell is no longer an egg. There were a few scraps of plastic hide still visible in the mess, and rags of clothing, but the rest was nothing but broken machinery: twisted steel frames, torn hanks of wiring, silent motors. A pool of hydraulic fluid spread slowly across the crazy paving. A false eyelash floated on it like a delicate water insect. I began to wish I were somewhere else.

'One down,' he said cheerfully. 'Four to go!' A line of black drool ran down his chin.

He started in at once on the tall short-order cook, whose name was Hatrack.

'Ouch! I wish you wouldn't do that, master. If you have to, okay, but – Ouch! I wish we could talk this over, master. Why don't I fix you a nice cup of java and a stack of buckwheat cakes and – Ouch!' After a while, Hatrack stopped saying ouch and dissolved into a second junkpile. One of his realistically bloodshot eyes glared up at the sky.

A little old woman, the Judge's wife, tottered out from the house with a glass of milk and a plate of cookies. 'Now you just sit down and have some refreshment, dear, before you do another thing. You're not as young as you used to be, one of these days you'll just faint and fall over in it, as we used to say.'

Meekly, the Judge sat down at a little white wrought-iron table and had his milk and cookies. His wife spoke, apparently to us. 'He doesn't take care of himself, you know. Still thinks he's young. Most men his age have a nap in the afternoon, but not him. No, he has to go swinging a crowbar and smashing up robots.'

'Why does he do it, ma'am?' I asked.

'Because he enjoys it, of course. It's his hobby, his little hobby. Keeps him busy and happy, and he's very good about clearing up the mess afterwards. A man has to have a hobby, doesn't he?'

'Okey-dokey,' said the Judge. He stood up, belched, and reached for his crowbar. His wife got out of the way quickly. In no time, there were two more little junkpiles.

'Sir,' I said in desperation, 'maybe you'd like to give me a sporting chance?'

'What kind of sporting chance?'

'A little head start, a couple of yards. And you could just chase me around the garden a few laps.'

'What would be the point? I'm going to demolish you anyway.' He raised the crowbar.

'Oh well, if you're feeling too *old* and *tired*—'

'Tired? I'll show you who's tired, ready get set, *go*!'

Our peculiar little race began. I hoped there was an outside chance that he might fall dead of a heart attack or something, or at least get too tired to kill me. Instead, I found the old boy to be a strong, sure runner, while my batteries began to drain. I heard his flapping footsteps coming closer and closer, and then, just before the crowbar ended my consciousness, I heard him say, '*You're it.*'

Since Teddy Roosevelt was one of Cord's heroes, I posed him next to a stuffed bear. Normally such a portrait would take me about an hour, but I had to pretend to have difficulty in capturing the signs of leadership which I pretended to find in his undistinguished face. It was in fact a face untroubled by any ideas or emotions, the face of a golfer. I knew this meant that he would soon be a general, and I was right. At our third sitting, I had to remove the gold arrows from his portrayed uniform and replace them with silver rosettes.

'Congratulations, general.'

'It means a move to Washington,' he sighed. 'But what the hell, a town's only as good as the people in it.'

'Or out of it,' I said, pretending to understand. I never understood his garbled maxims, if that's what they were, but I knew how to seem to reply to them.

'You got it, Tik-Tok, you got it. Intellectually, you're right on my wave beam, you know that? Not many human types are, it's funny I can get through to a robot. Guess it shows, there are robots vastly smarter than the massive herd of people. Too bad you can't come along to Washington, you're good for bouncing ideas off of. In fact—' He scribbled something on a card. 'In fact, if you ever feel like a little vacation from your owners and all this art stuff, give me a buzz at the Pentagon and I'll commandeer you.'

'Can that be done?'

'In the interests of National Security, anything can be done. I'm working at the top echelons, the top echelons. Liaising real close with the President on this.'

'No kidding?'

'The president has got his eye on yours truly, that's the frank truth of it, Tik-Tok. And you know how it is, when the President jumps . . .'

Cord made a grandiloquent, sweeping gesture with one arm and managed to rap his knuckles on the bear's teeth. I showed him to the bathroom to staunch the bleeding under cold water. Then, bandaids decorated with stars and stripes.

Up to that time, I'd never thought about politics.

The papers were full of stories about families of the air crash victims. I picked up a cheap home printer and knocked out a few letters like this:

Dear Mrs Smith:

So your husband and two kids died in that plane crash. Isn't it too bad. I bet you're all broke up, spending all that insurance money! Let's face it, the whole neighborhood knows how you and your hubby really got along. All I want to know is, who planted the bomb? Was it you, or the guy you been playing around with? Or did hubby find out the kids weren't his, and decide to finally get away from you?

If there was any justice, the government would have you hanged and burned alive and fed to stray dogs. I may run you over myself some night – be careful crossing the street! As for your three surviving kids, I wouldn't count on them growing up if I was you, ha ha. Killing's too good for them too, but I wouldn't mind hurting them real bad. Are you afraid of poisonous snakes? Be careful opening any packages for the rest of your miserable life!

– A Well-Wisher

Hard by the lake shore east of our city lay the campus of the University of Kiowa. Almost every building had been arranged to turn its back on the busy city and face the lake, together in a fair share of tranquillity. Now this choice was turning out to be a bad one. The lake was dead and putrefying, while the city – now that offices were vanishing – no longer seemed a threatening prospect. From here, the city's glittering towers now seemed monuments to a new heroic age, ruled by gods of light and metal and summer winds.

The University buildings no doubt glittered from a distance too, but close-up, the place seemed like a hostile camp under siege. Helmeted security guards were everywhere, some patrolling with large dogs, some with pumas. All were carrying sidearms, clusters of blackout gas grenades, and back packs large enough to hold riot guns. There was no sign of trouble, though students crossing the campus seemed to travel in larger crowds than necessary, as if convoying one another to classes.

Popper Hall was a conventional glass office building, from outside, whose academic function had been indicated by adding a sketch of a Greek temple facade, sketched in neon tubing. This was blue, indicating I suppose seriousness. Like all universities. Kiowa wanted to be taken seriously, but not too seriously. It craved the respect of intellectuals, but it wanted to become a part of 'society', too, an adjunct to the supermarket and the hamburger drive-in.

Inside the door, to the right, there was a small plaque with a quotation from Karl Popper:

A rationalist, as I use the word, is a man who attempts to reach decisions by argument and perhaps, in certain cases, by compromise, rather than by violence. He is a man who would rather be unsuccessful in consuming another man

64

by argument than successful in crushing him by force, by intimidation and threats, or even by persuasive propaganda.

–*Conjectures and Refutations*

Facing it, to the left, was an enormous billboard advertising motor oil. It showed a lush garden overgrown with poppies and mushrooms and orchids and ferns, and featuring also a lush nude. She lay prone, smiling and burying her face in a cluster of the same small flowers with which her hair was twined. The sun, or some glow from the sky, raised airbrushed highlights on her back and exaggerated buttocks. An oilcan in the sky was pouring oil over her legs and buttocks, and much had been made of the effects of light on this viscous, slightly fluorescent yellow-green liquid. A direct association of motor oil with sex, profane acts, nature's wonderland, mystical meanings – even the ambiguities of motor-oil 'dirtiness' – not bad. I could use a few painters like that in my stable, I thought, as I passed on up a white double staircase and through heavily guarded corridors to the seminar.

It was held in a tidy, colorless little conference room. Dr Riley sat at the far end of the table, apparently sleeping. Seven students lounged in their chairs, some pretending to read, others openly staring at me.

'Take a pew, Tik-Tok, and meet the gang,' said Riley. 'Nancy, Keith, Sybilla, Dean, Fent, Deedee, and Purina.'

There were nods from some, surly looks from others. The seminar began without further formality. Nancy delivered a paper on 'Robots, Mental States and Aesthetic Theory':

'It was Richard Wollheim who first proposed one kind of relationship between what an artist does and the artist's mental state. He said: 'If someone can recognize in something that he's made a reflection of an inner state, it is often the case that he would not have been aware of this state except through the object or objects that he makes. And one explanation of this can be that the mental state or condition, though in one sense remaining unchanged, has

65

acquired or developed a structure, a degree of inner articulation that it previously lacked.'

'If I may paraphrase what I think is this process, I would guess that it is somewhat like map-making. Each of an artist's works explores and charts a territory adjacent to others, or at least connected to others, that have gone before or will come later. The territory may be there before the map, but it is so hazily known as to have no useful existence.

'Suppose for example a painter produces two similar paintings – Rembrandt's self-portraits, say, or the naked and clothed Maja, or two views of Fujiyama. The two works together define a certain territory – perhaps the aesthetic space between them – which the painter now may understand is his to work within. Perhaps the first painting established his claim on this *terra incognita* and the second then goes on to push out the boundaries or merely goes over the details and improves the sharpness of the original map.

'There are several kinds of assumptions we could make about the inner landscape thus being externalized, or externally represented. We could assume that the painting is in some way entirely planned and modelled or painted within the inner landscape first, and that the painter simply transfers his plan to canvas. Or we could assume that everything happens during the execution of the real objective painting – the inner painting goes on at the same time. Or we could assume a kind of two-way traffic between the inner state and the outer painting, so that both reach finally some stability or stasis, at which point the painter decides his painting is finished.

'It can also be argued that what obtains for two paintings by one painter could obtain for two paintings by two painters, provided that they share enough common ground in their belief-states or ways of relating their work to the world. Hence *schools* or *movements* might be considered to be founded on partially shared inner landscapes.

66

'Until recently, however, all such assumptions about the relationship between the objective work and the subjective mental state have had little chance of testing. Now, the appearance of a robot who (or which) seems to paint in the same way humans paint, offers some fascinating possibilities. Unlike the human, the robot's mental state ought to be accessible to outsiders – at least in principle. In principle, then, it should be possible to probe that state in such a way as to be able to compare it, stage by stage, with the work that is actually being painted.'

I saw that all the others were awaiting my reaction. What I felt, though I wasn't showing it, was some anxiety. I decided to expel it in a joke.

'Probing, you say? I hope nobody's actually going to plunge a screwdriver into *my* head!' Moderate laughter.

Nancy, a pretty, chubby girl, showed a dimple. 'Not at all. I was only proposing a thought experiment, not an experiment on your thoughts.'

'Anyway, imagine philosophers being that practical,' said Keith, a thin boy in a wheelchair. 'Never heard of any philosophers settling anything by simply picking up a screwdriver.'

Riley asked for more questions, either of Nancy or me. A morose, pimply boy named Dean spoke first.

'Um, aren't we kind of moving too fast here? I mean um, Nancy's assuming the robot produces art before she finds out um what producing art is. I mean um couldn't it be just um a human activity? So that the canon of what is acceptable art has to be stuff that is the product of the human um imagination? Because in that case it's begging a question.'

Nancy shrugged. 'I guess in part the canon of what is acceptable has to be what critics accept, and they accept robot art. This doesn't mean you're wrong, Dean, though, because maybe robots are blessed with what we call human imagination. So ask Tik-Tok.'

I threw up my hands. 'This is all kind of fast-moving for me. I don't know whether to call my work art or not, but I feel there's a certain – what can I call it? Human element? – a certain human element in it. At least I hope there is. Because, though I know I never can be really human, I like to aim for humanity.' *With a great big nova bomb*, I thought. 'I guess we robots can't help but aspire to a condition of near-humanity, can we?'

This kind of speech, which in most circles makes people feel warm and friendly or even turned-on, seemed here to have little effect. One or two faces – the girl with pigtails, Sybilla – even registered disgust. Time to change direction. 'After all,' I added quickly, 'you folks have almost made it.'

A gasp from Deedee, but delighted grins from several others. Sybilla said, 'Almost is right. The one thing that's holding back humanity from becoming human now is the fact that we still want to keep slaves.'

Deedee said, 'I don't see why we all of a sudden have to bring politics into this. I for one didn't come here for a lecture on how all men are brothers, especially those with microchip brains.'

Judging by their clothes, I figured the conservatives in the class to be Deedee and Purina. Deedee alone wore a crisp sailcloth coat with matching eyeshade, but both wore traditional heavy makeup that included glued-on gold teardrops and fancy dental work. All in good taste.

Sybilla's appearance was at the other extreme. She wore no makeup; a garish, rainbow-striped shirt with wooden epaulets; natural hair with a blue fringe; and only one of her teeth had been capped with a light. Nancy and the boys also leaned towards this vulgarity, which would in twenty years probably become accepted good taste for another generation of conservatives.

Dr Riley, obscurely clothed as befits an arbiter, said, 'Why not politics? Philosophy should be able to handle anything, right?'

Sybilla said, 'Right! Deedee, just because you can't handle the idea of a robot having thoughts and feelings just as you have, doesn't mean the rest of us should restrict our discussion.'

'Sophistry,' said Deedee. 'Sophistry and cant!'

'Says you!'

A moment of silence ensued, during which Keith, turning his wheelchair slightly to face me, said, 'I wanted to put a question to our visitor about, er, moral constraints.'

Riley said, 'Fine, but try to keep it relevant to Nancy's paper.'

'Er, yeah well the idea of an inner landscape being mapped externally can work just as well if the landscape is ethical instead of aesthetic. In this case the subjective would be the conscience and the mapping doesn't produce works of art but acts which can be criticized on moral grounds. And again we have a robot model to test our ideas of this process on. So Tik-Tok, I want to ask you, if we assume you do have normal human thoughts and feelings, but we know you also have these special asimov circuits that are supposed to keep you from committing certain unethical acts, keep you from *sinning*, then do you feel as though you have free will?'

Inwardly, all my alarm bells were clanging away, but I kept telling myself that no one else realized how dangerous this game was. 'Keith, I'm not sure. I guess I do feel as though I have free will. So maybe the asimov circuits don't work like a human conscience. I guess a human conscience works kind of like a – an alarm system inside, right? So you think of doing something, and your conscience reminds you that it's wrong? Well my, uh, moral equipment doesn't work like that. It's more like, well, I never think of doing wrong in the first place. It just never occurs to me to say injure a human being. That's just not one of my choices. But within the choices I do have, I guess I'm free.'

'I don't understand that,' he said. 'If you're supposed to be built very close to human specifications, how can these asimov circuits work at all? I mean, you get angry, don't you? At people?'

'Oh, sure.'

'But you never get angry enough to take a punch at anybody?'

'I might.' I attempted a shrug. 'But actually taking a punch

69

never crosses my mind. I guess I'm a pacifist.'

Indulgent chuckles all around. Riley said, 'I think we ought to start winding this up. One point I think somebody might have brought up following on from Nancy's paper is the aesthetic status of robots themselves. She pointed out that there are schools and movements in art, in which a number of artists can be said to share parts of the same inner landscape. The concept of creating robots does seem to be an old, persistent and widespread one. Maybe robots are the mapping of a broad and deep inner landscape – or seascape? In any case, robots certainly live in *our* aesthetic space, so what they produce – what Tik-Tok produces – might be considered a kind of secondary elaboration: a work of art which produces out of its own inner world, works of art. Who's going to mess around with that idea for next week? Fent?'

After class, Sybilla steered me along the hall. 'Listen, I just want you to know we're not all like old Riley.'

'Oh?'

'Like at the last minute there, when he tries to sneak in a way of denying the validity of your work. What he really wants to say is, robots are nothing but *objets d'art*, so we don't have to consider them as in any way human. It's all part of the old game, denying robots the products of their own labor, their own minds.'

'I didn't realize that.'

'And it makes me damned mad. Tik-Tok, if you've got a few minutes. I know a few people who would like to meet you. I mean, you seem really *free*.'

She took me into a kind of Common Room and introduced me to a small band of students wearing WAGES FOR ROBOTS buttons. I saw at once that they were waiting for me to approve of them, give them guidance and advice, or even lead them.

They had drawn up some vinyl-covered chairs in a semi-circle around a coffee table. There were two more chairs for Sybilla and me. Ignoring mine, I put a foot on the coffee table, leaned over and glared at these innocent revolutionaries.

'Well here I am, meatfaces,' I roared. 'Take a good look.

Count the damn rivets! Check the damn circuit diagram! Read the damn serial number! Make sure there's a five-year warranty! And when you get all done making sure I'm the real thing, you can kiss my copper-plated ass!'

They all fell back against their vinyl, Sybilla included. Someone started to make a feeble protest, and I looked at him.

'Yes? Something wrong? Did I forget my place, little master?'

'No, gee, I just thought—'

'You thought! You thought! You thought meat thoughts with your meat head! You thought crap thoughts with your crap head! You think meat crap and therefore you are meat crap! You're in my world, now, my world. No more smiling robot slaves running to wipe your nose and say nice things to soothe your meat ego. I want you to see my world, the robot world. You know what robots think of you behind your back? You know what we call you? *Shitbellies*, that's what we call you. Shitbellies, you want to be my brothers and sisters?'

They said yes.

'Well you can't, not yet. Because there's two big differences between you and me. You got two things I ain't. You got power and you got bellies full of shit.'

I had learned preaching from the Reverend Flint Orifice himself! Yes, the same whistle-sweet young-old man now known to millions for his talk show, *Voice in the Wilderness*. Of course what you see today is a robot double; it's been some time now since the real Reverend Flint died. I was with him at the end, just as he was with me when I died. And when I was born again.

After Judge Arnott laid into me with that crowbar, I was dead or near enough, but I was not smashed into a non-robot. Probably chasing me tired the old fellow out, for he contented himself with two or three blows smashing in my skull. I was then taken away and dumped in an alley, where Reverend Flint found me. In those days he scoured the alleys for both human flotsam and robot jetsam, wrecks to reclaim and put to work for the Lord.

71

I awoke on a workbench in a sunny room. A person wearing real glasses was grinning at me as he or she probed my open stomach with a screwdriver.

'How you feeling today, fella?'

'Could be worse,' I said. 'After a beating like that, I'm surprised there's enough of me left to feel anything. Where am I, anyway? Is this some kind of reconditioning depot? I hope you're not going to junk me, because I'm a hard worker and trained in kitchen duties.'

That was what I tried to say, but I heard my voice saying instead:

'Clead bo wilted rarf llo *Beid bi Tom* ala Trapp. He'g spatial-temporal althir embolismus o' matrix arm leaffolds ampers! Wage annointed aurochs – special angles make light Egyptian brown beans – clead be willed – clead – acute? Is't treat som'll kohlrabi the old Ra drayperson? I hope not. I hope you'm gluten sender's jump-seat coriander or other (*ton* in kerchiefed gack?). Selah, mac. Errant frisbee-like slung post office be ne'er so insert, noday?'

'He's speaking in tongues,' my interlocuter said to someone I could not see.

'I could use that. Can you keep it on ice?'

'Nothing easier, Rev. We just cock in a modal switch here, neatsfoot el Strabo, signalize and you're in broadloom salt.'

'Plinks. Let's radish the restaurant for vote?'

Evidently the distortions affected my hearing at times, too. But now the person at my belly made an adjustment and suddenly the world was too clear. I turned my head to look into the kindly gray eyes of Reverend Flint.

'*Me*! I mean *you*!'

'Recognize me, do you, son?'

'Everybody knows you, you're the resurrection man.'

'I am the resurrection and the life, but it surely do cost money.' He smiled the now-famous smile. 'I hope you'll stick around and help in God's good work?'

As if I had a choice. A robot found abandoned was of course the property of the finder, by the laws of salvage.

My work was easy enough. Reverend Flint at that time

moved from town to town, giving live performances with only the occasional telecast. I was equipped with weeping machinery and a memorized confession and planted in the audience. At some critical moment in each performance, I would leap to my feet and shout: 'I have sinned, yes Lord! I have sinned, yes Lord!'

Reverend Flint would say, 'Brother, lay it on the Lord. Fess up and your sins are forgave you.'

'O Lord I started out with everything: a good job driving truck, a loving wife and two fine children. And I lost everything – I – I—' Here I turned on the weeping.

'Go on, brother, spit it out.'

'First it was just a little social drinking at the bowling alley . . .' The story was patched together from various country songs, already tested for popularity. I took the wife's wedding ring off the sink and sold it for whisky money. I beat her, starved the kids, lost jobs. Finally one day I drove my 180-ton rig blind drunk, and ran over my two darling children. I knelt on the running board and asked the Lord to take my life too.

Usually this was enough to limber up a congregation, but if they needed more, I would then press the button on my naval and speak in tongues. I could say anything, such as 'No business like showbusiness, eh Rev? And look at this mob of sweaty rubes. I hope you dry-clean their money before you touch it,' and so on, and it would always come out 'Clead bo wilted rarf,' etc.

No one ever seemed to suspect I was a plant, let alone a planted robot. Life was slow, but sweet enough, and I even thought of finding Gumdrop and sending for her, now that I had a steady job. But of course it was too good to last.

Lint was our undoing. Not having had a naval before, I didn't realize that it would accumulate lint, requiring daily harvesting. Lint jammed my pentecostal button, so that I pressed it and blurted out, without thinking, 'Okay, Rev, let down your nets and pull up some cash. You know, when I look around at all these Neanderthals, I'm not surprised they don't believe in evolution. Most of 'em have got enough fingers to count their own IQs – twelve. If God loved the common people so much, as Lincoln said, how come He made them so common? And ugly? I—'

Lint and charisma were our undoing. Reverend Flint's great organization was not going to be stopped by a little incident like this. Flint had a contingency plan ready, and now it went into action. A woman in the audience was to stand up at a signal and fire a blank pistol at Reverend Flint. He would then clap a bladderful of fake blood to his eye and fall down on the stage. An ambulance would whisk him away as the show closed – both to be revived when any trouble blew over.

The woman was signalled. She stood up and fired, but not blanks. Reverend Flint Orifice was killed instantly.

'I killed him because I loved him,' Irma Jeeps said at her trial. 'I've always loved him. I joined his crusade two years ago just to be near him, and ever since then I've been working my way up, until I got to be one of his secretaries. It was enough just to see him every day. But then when he chose *me* to fire the gun, I knew he felt the same. He wanted me to kill him so we could be together for eternity.'

It turned out she'd felt the same about other charismatic figures. Irma had been arrested for attempts on the lives of the French singer Louis de la Renault and the handsome young Senator from Indiana. She had been caught armed, breaking into the palatial home of Dr Otto, the popular diet consultant (remember the 'Innsbruck Whey' diet?). And she had applied for a job as secretary to Dr Lugné-Poe, the most famous obstetrician of our age. It was he who proposed that women give birth in the natural manner of bats, hanging upside down in totally dark caves. Irma Jeeps was actually offered a job as his secretary and probably Dr Lugné-Poe would be dead today, had he not been exposed as a fraud. One Sunday paper carried scandalous pictures of his patients having babies *in comfortable beds under ordinary lighting conditions*. That week, Irma Jeeps turned down the job.

The Reverend Flint Orifice Crusade recovered from the death of its leader. It went on television with a robot double and a largely hired congregation (why take chances?). There was now no room for me in the showbiz side of the operation, and I was an embarrassing reminder of bad luck. So they sent me on a mission to Mars.

When I finished with the Wages for Robots students, they were almost too stunned to thank me for my abuse. A couple of the girls, and one of the boys, wanted to go to bed with me. Someone wanted to talk about Marx, someone compared me to Jesus Christ and Pancho Villa, there was talk about talk and talk about action. I saw that only two of the group were worth wasting time on: Sybilla White who had practical political ideas, and a skinny lad called Harry LaSalle, who was studying law.

Sybilla said, 'Listen, TT, the political temperature is going up on this campus and on other campuses. Right now the big issues are the Martian war and our dying economy, but I see Wages for Robots coming up fast. One of these days the damn war will be over, and people can't relate to the economy alone. Robots are a natural for the next key issue. Will you help us?'

'What can I do?' I said. 'You know if I make too many waves, it's easy for them to shut me up. I don't know if I'm martyr material.'

She didn't seem disappointed. 'I understand. All I want now is your *secret* commitment to the cause. You don't have to support us openly until it's safe – and I know we can make it safe.'

Harry nodded. 'I've looked at these movements in the past. Within about three to five years, we'll either peter out or get major legislation shoved through. I think the first steps will be state laws allowing robots to earn money and own property. But it'll end up with a Constitutional amendment guaranteeing robot civil rights.'

Those state laws sounded promising. 'I wonder if I could find some way around the property laws now?' I asked. 'If so, I could be donating money to your group.'

Sybilla and Harry looked pleased. He said. 'You could get

your earnings put into a trust fund, administered by your own corporation.'

'But how can I have a corporation?'

'The same way a child or a dog has one. You have no control, but the whole arrangement is for your care and protection. Look, if you're interested, I'll get my dad working on it. He knows everything there is to know about trust funds, I'm sure he can come up with something.'

I took my leave and ambled along the corridor, daydreaming about corporate power. Ahead of me, at the top of the double staircase, I saw Keith in his wheelchair. He was just negotiating the first broad step on his way down.

'Keith!' I cried. 'Let me help you.'

'No. No, I—'

But I was already rushing forward to give the chair a sharp kick. It vaulted forward, careened off a marble balustrade and took a somersault down the last flight to crack its occupant's head noisily on the floor below.

A security guard rushed over and seized my arm. 'This is the one! I saw him push him over!' he shouted. I relaxed and waited.

The crowd moved in close around us. 'That's ridiculous,' said someone. 'Officer, you got a robot there.'

'Hey, it's Tik-Tok! They got Tik-Tok!' People started jostling us and shouting abuse at the guard.

Sybilla broke through. 'I saw it all, Keith was falling and Tik-Tok just ran forward to save him. What kind of frame-up is this?'

The guard suddenly dropped my arm. 'Fuck it, then, I ain't paid enough.' He pushed away through the mob of faces, some jeering, some cheering, but none looking at the dead man down below.

In the awful art gallery on the ground floor were now 'Rubbings of Serbian Radios' along with 'Mouth-Paintings to Jazz: a Retrospective'. I felt as thought the staleness of that place had somehow seeped up to my studio and into me. I had nothing to do.

My studio now took up all the upper floors of the building. Nobby ran the painting teams almost without me, on three floors. Below him, Blojob spent his time cleaning guns and repairing old military robots (stacking weapons where once the cheese sculptor had stacked fragrant materials). Another floor was becoming an unofficial office for Wages for Robots, and another was ready to be business quarters when my corporation took over (if ever). For now, politics and business seemed to have stalled.

Hornby wasn't throwing any parties. I tried wandering down to the levée to watch the rohobos die, but the sun was hot. I went to the public library, but just now there was nothing I wanted to read. I managed to force myself to play one game of chess with the nasty old man in Nixon Park, but the sun was too hot. I went back to the studio.

'Blojob, let's get the game afoot.'

'Yes boss?'

'What kind of troops do you have here?'

He marched a few out and showed me. 'Heavy assault stuff', boss. Good armor, heat-resistant, they can run, climb, bust down doors and fall on their heads without damage. Then I got security stuff, not so mobile but better at defense. Coupla missile carriers, a coupla general-purpose anti-personnel monsters—'

'What do they do?'

'A little of everything. Between them, they can throw flames, spit acid, shoot dum-dums and riot guns, fill a room with mustard gas, rip through a crowd with hooks or knives, explode white phosphorus, shrapnel or darts, do concussion blasts, emit amplified screams, look tough. They're real handy, Boss. Dress 'em up in black leather with brass studs all over it, they can serve a subpoena anywhere.'

'Okay then, here's what we'll do. I want us to stick up a - I mean, we're making a video about sticking up a jewelry store. But the video has to be very, very realistic. So all the cameras will be kept out of sight.'

'No kidding.'

'And I want us to use real weapons and do everything for real, okay?'

'Anything "you" say, Boss.' Blojob had an annoying habit of putting the word 'you' in quotes, as though to remind me that my orders were really just passed on from some invisible master. His smugness was unbearable. It was the smugness of certain Christians in their Christian certainty, the smugness of Deacon Cooper.

Deacon Copper and I, missionaries to Mars, took passage on the freighter *Doodlebug*. The voyage was like a dream, beginning and ending nowhere. At the Darkblaze Travel Agency, a little, unshaven man with gold teeth explained that we would need to be unconscious for the takeoff – something to do with adjusting to the ship's artificial gravity, he said. He gave Deacon Cooper a shot of something to put him to sleep right there in the office. Then he turned off my senses.

Deacon woke me in our cabin. 'We're on our way! Mars or bust! This is it, our greatest mission!'

Busting seemed a possibility, from what I could see of the *Doodlebug*: flickering lights, paint peeling from rusting bulkheads, every surface covered with dirt and grease.

The captain, when he came to see us, did not exactly inspire confidence, either. He was a large, unshaven man (without gold teeth) in a rumpled uniform. His smile was tentative, and he kept looking over his shoulder.

'My name is Captain Reo. Just wanted to make sure you're comfortable, Deacon. And your robot.'

'We're fine, captain, fine. Great! Hey, when do we make port?'

'In about eight hundred and fifty days.'

'Any other passengers on board?'

'Yes, yes, the um Jord family. But they um stay in their cabin a lot.' He looked over his shoulder. 'I think they're um Martians. Kind of um rough diamonds, heh heh.'

'Fine, great, fine,' said Deacon. 'I imagine we'll see them at mealtimes, eh? At the Captain's table?'

'The Captain's table? Well, Deacon, as you know, the Reverend Flint Orifice Crusade paid the basic fare, which covers you and um—' he looked at me – 'and all cabin luggage. But it doesn't cover food. So if you want to pay now, I'll be glad to have you dine at my table.'

Deacon grinned. 'I ain't got a dime, Captain. Just a suitcase full of pamphlets and a spare paper collar.'

The captain grinned back. 'No money? You can always work in the galley. We have a hungry crew, and the cook will be glad to get some help.'

Deacon looked at me. 'My assistant here could work in my place, couldn't he? He has kitchen experience.'

'No!' The captain looked behind him. 'This is a *union* ship. My crew may seem like ignorant Lapps to you, but they work union rules. If I let one robot lift one finger on board, the whole crew walks out. Probably lose my ticket. Nope, it has to be you, Deacon.'

So it was that, while Deacon Cooper slaved long hours in the galley, I had the run of the ship and enough leisure to enjoy the voyage.

The *Doodlebug* was supposed to be a Liberian-registered cattle boat, carrying a small herd of dairy cows and some vats of cattle embryos in suspended animation. The latter could be kept indefinitely, then reconstituted and raised as needed.

But there were other parts of the ship that had nothing to do with cattle. I found a cobwebbed ballroom with dusty gilt chairs, for example, and a giant Gents' room with marble walls and sinks, two barber chairs and a shoeshine stand. There was a 'First Class Only' coffee room where brocaded sofas rotted near the collapsed carcase of a grand piano. It was there I found a rosewood writing desk, and in the back of its

79

drawer a supply of notepaper headed *SS Dolly Edison*. This meant nothing to me at the time.

There was also an incomparable library where I spent long weeks reading and viewing. There was no fixed pattern to my reading. For a time I chose only books in which robots named Robbie appeared. Then I read only the autobiographies of ex-nuns. For a whole week I sampled items whose titles begin with U, those titles often seeming to conceal profane meanings:

> Donald Barthelme, *Unspeakable Practices, Unnatural Acts*
> George Gissing, *The Unclassed*
> Malcolm Lowry, *Ultramarine* ·
> Harriet Beecher Stowe, *Uncle Tom's Cabin*
> Thomas Nashe, *The Unfortunate Traveller*
> Charles Dickens, *The Uncommercial Traveller*
> Robert Records, *The Urinal of Physick*
> Vasko Popa, *Unrestfield*
> Nell Dunn, *Up the Junction*
> Iris Murdoch, *Under the Net*
> Dorothy L. Sayers, *The Unpleasantness at the Bellona Club*
> Thomas More, *Utopia*

Inevitably, I began studying Mars and the Martians. In his spare moments, Deacon joined me to watch videos of ugly people living in tin shacks that clung grimly to the soil of an unloved place. Mars had never had much to offer in the way of water or oil or even dirt. Any natural beauty it might once have had now lay concealed behind billboards, neon-lit casinos, auto graveyards, dark forests of wells, bright gashes of mining operations, files of giant pylons bringing power to seas of ugly little houses.

The Martians were not without religion, we learned. There were over 23,000 registered sects in the main population centers, ranging from the exotic (Hermetic Lodge of the Ninth Zoroastrian Affinities) to the familiar (Church of Christ Dry Cleaner – Alterations While U Wait; First Church of the Snodgrass Family of 112 Oakland Avenue West).

Every other house seemed to be some kind of tabernacle. The television channels were clogged with ranters, chanters, rollers, healers. A Bible was probably being thumped, somewhere on Mars, every two seconds.

'It all signifieth nothing,' said Deacon. His own hand (cracked and bleeding from washing dishes) made an automatic Bible-thumping gesture. 'If these people ain't been saved by the Reverend Flint Orifice Crusade, they ain't been saved at all. We all got to throw down and break all these false idols, so the good folk of Mars can see the light.'

Our main enemy was a popular creed called Reformed Darwinism, which came about through an accident of history. At the time the colony was being established, a debate was going on in America over the controversial claims of someone called Charles Darwin, a foreigner. Darwin evidently claimed that animals evolved, one species turning into another. This was supposed to happen by means of 'natural selection', in which the fittest members of a species survive, while the less fit perish. The question was, was this science?

It was found in some states that the real guardians of science and scientific truth were religious leaders and lawyers, unswayed by facts. Scientists were generally so dogmatic and arrogant as to claim that some fact were just facts and not matters of religious preference at all.

The debate raged on until the turn of the century, when some of the more anti-Darwin sects lost a lot of their steam. Many of them had been counting on the end of the world in 1999. When it didn't end, a great many of their flock stopped putting money in the collection plates and took up hobbies: fishing, car-washing, TV criticism.

But then a counter-sect arose, embracing persons who thought they believed in Darwin's novel theory. What they actually believed in was Reformed Darwinism, a religious and social theory combining 'survival of the fittest' with 'Devil take the hindmost'. The important thing was to be a survivor. Take care of your tribe and your territory. Be selfish. God helps those who help themselves.

To the new Martian colonists, this seemed a tailor-made religion. They lived where tribalism and selfishness really counted, where territory was money. Many of them had already served prison sentences for selfish acts. Reformed Darwinism captured their hearts and rudimentary minds.

'This is going to be tough,' said Deacon Cooper. 'We have to make our message look good to people who would kill each other for a plastic harmonica.'

'Are we going to tell them how Jesus said we should all love one another and—'

'No, definitely not. That's the last thing they want to hear. We got to show them, I don't know, I guess that Jesus Christ was the toughest guy on the block. I looked up a few gospel items here, there's the story of how he's sitting there with his gang one day and a woman comes up and pours some expensive after-shave over him, and the other guys say shouldn't we be giving money to the poor instead of wasting it like this? Only he says, 'Forget the poor, the poor you have always with you, there's always somebody with their hand out.' And I found other passages where it says he owned his own house, he paid his taxes and he wasn't a scrounger. Now if we can just link our message to Martian life-style thinking . . .'

'If only we could talk to the Jord family, Deke.'

But Vilo Jord and his kin never came on deck. We found ourselves, like anthropologists in pursuit of a lost tribe, trying to reconstruct the Martians we'd never met from all available information, even from fiction. One old novel claimed that Martians shared water; we knew they shared nothing. Another novel had them playing German batball; we found their game of preference to be softball.

'I don't see why we shouldn't use a lot of softball metaphors,' said Deacon. 'Say the pitcher's mound is Calvary, runners on first and third are the good thieves, Judas Iscariot is the cleanup batter, the rosin bag is gall and vinegar, and so on.' He sat studying his cracked, bleeding hands for a moment. 'And so on.' We'd been aboard the *Doodlebug* for more than a month, now, and the Deacon had begun to crack in other ways. Was there a pitcher's mound in softball?

The idea of spending time among the Martians was beginning to lose its appeal, as we read on: They were mainly rough, uncouth men with no imagination, no ambition, no money. They all lived in tiny suburban bungalows – metal outside, paperframe inside – with 'colonial' façades. Usually such a house would have a bong tree in the glassed-in front yard, which was called a *godden*. Bong trees were sickly items, but much prized on Mars. They were four-foot yellow spindles producing a few needles and a few large yellow pods, empty as the rest of Martian life.

The house itself, called a *teep*, usually had three rooms: kitchen, bedroom and sickroom. Because of the handling of mined minerals, no less than the constant drinking and drugs, it was necessary to have one room which could be cleaned very easily, the sickroom or *barfy*. If the house had a fourth room, it was the garage. Martians spend a lot of time with their cars.

Before we tackled videos of the actual Martians talking about their lives, we first had to learn their language. It was an American dialect, spoken with a North Iowa accent, but the vocabulary had undergone deep changes: Mars or Martian was now *Marty*; a man was a *brudda* or a *Marty-brudda*; a woman was a *snap*. Food was *spew*; dinner was *grabbin the barf-bag*; a car was a *goodwheel* or a *can*; whiskey was *Budapest*; gin was *goose*; beer was *parthenogenesis*; all amphetamine related drugs were *monkey bread*; antidepressants were *furze*; tranquillizers were *Circassian chicken*; sleeping pills were *weenies*; cola drinks of any type were *jissom*; poison capsules (sold openly and quite legally in the colony) were *Sylvesters*; a hand-scrubbed floor was a *murph*; wages were *greengage*; racing imaginary horses was *purplesnow*; a message from Earth was a *plywooder*. Knuckle keys, for some reasons, were called *wurpy*.

One day the Deacon was jubilant (*serrated*). 'I've really cracked this language barrier, you know? I mean I've really, really cracked it. I can communicate, I can get right inside the head and guts of these people, you know? Know thy enemy, like. I mean I can finally cut through the bullshit (*quidge*) and talk to them. That means some chance of really converting them.

'Listen, you've been really helpful here, I'm gonna do something for you in return. You work for the Crusade for just one year after we land, and I'll turn you loose.'

'Turn me loose?'

'On Mars, there are free robots. The cook told me. They can work and earn wages just like any free human being! Oh, I tell you, there's a glorious day a-coming!' He waved his hideous hands, now coverd with pus and weeping sores. I saw that the Deacon was feverish, probably delirious. I began to hate him, if hate is the word. Even in his pain he had to be smug, making promises that could not be kept. Either he would turn out to be wrong (no free robots on Mars) or he would die before freeing me. Either way I would end my days grubbing away on the ugliest planet, watched among people who talked like those on the video we now watched.

FIRST MARTIAN: *Grok, brudda.*

(Hello, fellow Martian.)

SECOND MARTIAN: *Grokola, Marty-brud. My parsnip is fraughter nor a dead skate's greep, ow you?*

(Hello. I could use a drink, how about you?)

FIRST MARTIAN: *Too wry, nuncle. Not schlepped the old barf-bag since the old snap jived earthside, curd shore use a spew and a pinter pipi.*

(Right. I haven't dined out since my girl left me, so I could sure use a meal and a beer.)

SECOND MARTIAN: *Bow-wow. There is no ankle-grine without some wallop a frigstore ending. Me got brakes, let's scop the joot so snaffle a coupla pinters.*

(Fine. Every stone must have its well. I've got a car, let's ?? the road and grab two beers.)

84

While we were still puzzling over *scop*, an alarm siren went off somewhere in the ship. The *Doodlebug* always had some kind of alarm going off – being a big ship and old – but this time the captain spoke to us over the PA system:

'Attention all passengers and crew, this is the captain speaking. We are um being um spacejacked – is that the word?' There was the sound of machinegun fire. 'Hijacked, okay, we're being hijacked. By the um Vilo Jord and Family Liberation Front.' There was a long pause, and then he said, 'That is all. Thank you.'

From time to time we heard gunfire from distant parts of the ship.

The Deacon's eyes were shining. 'Real Martys! This Jord family are real Martys! This is our chance to try out the lingo. Let's go.'

'Go, boss?' I began to feel uneasy.

'We won't find them sitting here. Come on, grab some pamphlets and follow me.'

'But isn't it dangerous?'

'God laughs at danger,' he said, quoting one of the pamphlets he was now stuffing into his pockets. 'Get the lead out.'

I was more worried about keeping it out, but there was nothing to do but obey. I collected an assortment of Crusade pamphlets:

Christ had short hair!

Is Heaven enough? (The answer was No; after getting to Heaven it was necessary to get a house in a good neighborhood.)

The Reverend Flint Orifice Story

Double Tithing – the best investment!

Zither fish fools scientists – God laughs!

Caesarian birth: myth or reality?

We heard more gunfire as we stepped out into the companionway. 'Deacon, are you sure this is the smart thing to do? Maybe they're killing people. Those can't all be warning shots.'

85

'Don't worry,' he said. '*We* speak the lingo!'

As he spoke, we turned a corner and found our first body. The ship's carpenter lay face-up at the foot of a ladder. His chest was full of bullet-holes and his face was curiously mutilated.

On the upper deck we found two more bodies of crewmen, again with facial mutilations. Deacon bent over one, checking the cigar in its hand. 'Still warm. We're getting close.'

We hurried down greasy iron steps into the hold, an enormous barrel of a room with a ceiling forty metres above us in the greasy gloom. Along the curved walls, cattle hung in hammocks. There were a dozen of these Bossies, each in its own floral print hammock or sling, with a separate smaller hammock for its udder. The horns were protected by transparent globes of hardened glass. Since these cattle were all Holsteins, the room was filled at all times with accordion music. As we came in, the creatures were swaying gently to the *Minneapolis Polka*.

On the floor were the cylindrical glass tanks of cattle embryos. Each glowing tank held ten gallons, or enough little cows to populate the Milky Way, I understood. There were 28 in all, each throbbing with a different color of light, for identification: red for Jersey, orange for Guernsey, etc.

As we made our way silently down the ladder to floor level, we could see a group of armed people by the vats. Their savage faces and gleaming weapons reflected the glow from a red-blue (Jersey-Angus) tank, as they tapped it into plastic tankards. Rude laughter echoed over the accordion music.

I tugged at the Deacon's sleeve and whispered: 'Maybe we shouldn't disturb them just now, boss. If we wait a while, maybe they'll be in a better mood.'

'Wait? Never!' he said aloud. I heard automatic weapons being cocked. The shadowy figures all turned to face us.

Deacon Cooper marched towards them, holding out a fistful of pamphlets. 'Grok, bruddas! Your parsnip must be fraughter nor a dead skate's greep, so snaffle a coupla pinters, yo?'

'Stay where you are. Don't come any closer!'

'Pax, Marty-bruddas, Marty-snaps. Got great plywooder of God!' he said, bearing down on them. 'God howdys those who howdy themselves! Me avalanche plywooder-kid of Reverend Flint Orifice Crusade, God say let the serration—'

One of the figures shot him, and he fell in a flurry of tracts. The assassin stooped to cut off the Deacon's nose and add it to the hideous collection on his belt. 'What the Christ kinda lingo was he talking, anyways?'

One of the other figures aimed a weapon at me. 'There's another one.'

'Don't shoot!' I said. 'I'm a robot, and I could be useful.'

'Come over here slowly.' I did so. 'Okay, useful, suppose you tell me why this here piña colada tastes like elephant pee?'

'Not for drinking,' I explained. 'It's a solution of cattle embryos.'

'Aw jeez, we thought it was premixed cocktails.' Someone opened up on the vats, putting out their lights and murdering trillions of invisible cows. The real cows above us lowed, complaining of the noise that interrupted their *Lady of Spain.*

At dusk, Blojob and the gang brought in a steel drum full of spoils for my inspection.

'Any casualties?'

'It went like a dream, Boss. Oh, we picked up a couple bullet holes here and there, nothing serious. And like "you" ordered, we didn't leave no witnesses.'

'Excellent.' I peered into the drum. It was three-quarters full of jewelry, mostly platinum and gold on top with a few diamonds gleaming in the depths. 'Quite a haul for a first attempt.'

Blojob said, 'Thanks, Boss, but it ain't jest as good as it looks, there's some junk in there too, underneath.'

'Junk? Costume jewelry?'

'Naw, you know, odds and ends. Coupla velvet trays, some busted glass, a few fingers and one or two hands. We ain't had a chance to clean it up yet.'

'A very successful video,' I said. 'All very realistic. I think we'll probably make a few more, maybe a bank job or a bullion job. Yes, we'll make a lot more.'

'Whatever "you" say, Boss.'

'Just take a good look, meatfaces. Count the damn rivets! Check the damn circuit diagram! Read the damn serial number! Make sure there's a five-year warranty! And when you get all done making sure I am the real thing, you can kiss my copper-plated ass!'

It always seemed to work. There was a couple of hundred Wages for Robots people in the auditorium, applauding at every insult. When I had finished calling them shitbellies, they cheered themselves hoarse.

After all the questions, it was late. Sybilla White and Harry LaSalle walked with me to my limousine which, for obvious reasons, couldn't collect me at the door.

'The temperature is hotting up all over the country,' Sybilla said. 'Wages for Robots is going to be a key issue in election year. And already four states have passed interim bills giving limited rights to robots.'

'It's a big international issue,' said Harry. 'The Swedes are drafting a full citizenship law right now, and there were those big demonstrations last week in Japan, France and Germany. The German cops used blackout gas, now they've got a hundred and fifty students in the hospital.'

Sybilla said, 'Yeah, but in France the cops not only beat up students, they went around later smashing robots. Anywhere they caught a robot on the street, they just—'

'Yeah,' said Harry. 'But hey listen, TT, my dad says he's found a way for you to form your corporation. I'm supposed to take you to his office tomorrow at eleven, is that okay? In the Boregard Tower. So I'll meet you downstairs at ten forty-five.'

I arrived at the imposing entrance of Boregard Tower at exactly ten forty-five the following morning, stepped out of my limousine and stood for a moment admiring the great building. Boregard Tower is a tall green sliver of glass, out of which seem to grow great eyeballs in clusters. These eyes, scattered over its whole surface, are of all possible types – brown to violet, bluish whites to bloodshot jaundice, myopic and so on – but all are made to turn and gaze steadily at the sun throughout the day.

A handcuff was clamped on my wrist. Someone showed me a badge. Two tired-looking middle-aged men seized my arms.

'But what are you arresting me for?'

'Suspicion. Get in the car.' There was no chance to resist; they were very efficient, lifting and dragging me into the car. One of them crowded me on either side.

'Suspicion of what? You know I'm a robot.'

One of them said, 'Suspicion of kidnapping.' The other one snickered. It was at that moment I realized that they weren't policemen.

Sure enough, they put a bag over my head and pushed me down on the floor, where they used me for a footrest. I spent the rest of the journey trying to count the right and left turns, but getting mixed up. At last we stopped in a place that sounded like woodland, judging by the excess of bird noises. I was led stumbling through dirt, up a rough step and through a door. A voice that I seemed to remember said:

'Good work. Take the bag off him then, let's see if he looks worth ten million.'

I was in a log cabin, facing a rough wooden desk. On the wall to my right was a dartboard, to my left, deer-antlers. On the wall behind the desk was a calendar from a funeral parlor. Below it a man sat tapping his cigarette into a curious ashtray.

'Smilin' Jack,' I said.

'Banjo!'

'What are you doing here?' we said in unison.

George 'Smilin' Jack' Grewney was one of the hijackers who stood there in the gloomy hold, watching the dreary rain of cowshit, listening to *Lady of Spain*. It was he who said, 'No drink. I knew we should have hijacked a passenger ship.'

'We couldn't afford the fares, remember?'

'We've hijacked nothing! Nothing! The ship itself isn't

worth the cowshit on the floor here,' said Grewney. 'And now, no drink!'

'Ladies and gentlemen,' said the voice of Captain Reo. He was trussed up and hanging from a ladder above us. 'I have a few bottles of grog in my cabin. Please accept them with the compliments of the management. And now if you'll release me, I'll take you wherever you want to go'. I noticed that Captain Reo was wearing spurs.

When they'd collected the grog, someone said, 'Hey you. Banjo. Show us where we can sit down and enjoy life.'

I, Banjo, led them to the grand ballroom, whose pathetic decay only heightened the sense of unattainable grandeur. It reminded me of Tenoaks and the Culpeppers, and I realized that once more I was to be a proper servant to a new leisured class. The barbarian gentry made themselves right at home, and in no time were roasting a cow over a fire of gilt chairs.

The 'Jord Family' were no family at all, merely a gang of cutthroat adventurers. While I could not approve of their methods, I could not help admiring their courage and gruff, good-natured camaraderie. In another time and place they might have been musketeers, privateers, Sherwood Foresters, winners of the West, mercantile bankers.

There was Vilo Jord himself, a former attaché of the Chilean consulate at Las Vegas until accused and recalled for various offenses – the least of which was impersonating an orthodontist. Jord was a tall, stooped man with a heavy moustache, which he dyed a bilious green.

There was George 'Smilin' Jack' Grewney, a gum-chewing aristrocrat with a ready grin and a glass eye. A former undertaker, Grewney had been convicted of three premature burials, also of numerous ashtray and lampshade crimes.

The apple-cheeked twins, Fern and Jean Worpne, claimed to be wanted in eight countries for the mercy-killing of judges.

The scholarly-looking Jack Wax, wanted for engaging in illicit sexual behavior with telephone poles, seemed harmless enough by comparison with Sherm Chimini, the 'Armpit Rapist'. Sherm's otherwise engaging smile was marred by the presence of one abnormal incisor, four inches long, curved and barbed.

He in turn was hardly as frightening in appearance as Jud Nedd, a fat, effeminate man with motionless eyes, a man who specialized in public animal explosions. He it was who sabotaged an international canine frisbee-catching contest by introducing frisbees of his own hellish design, set to explode when caught. Only the clumsiest dog survived.

Duke Mitty, an avuncular toad usually drunk and giggling, had begun as a salesman of tapeworm cures, but later turned to the disposal of unwanted infants to sausage factories.

Finally, Maggie Dial, known as the Bitch of Brownsville, had amassed her unlawful fortune in Texas by impersonating animals in an outlawed variety of psychodrama. Patients taking rôles in these plays were heavily drugged and hypnotized in order to convince them that they were embracing the Egyptian animal gods of old. In fact these were ordinary sheep, dogs, owls and (playing all dangerous roles) Maggie.

In sentencing her, the judge described Maggie's crimes as 'distasteful to the bulk of Texas society'. Ironically, a sudden liberalization of Texas laws made the forbidden form of psychodrama not only permitted but respectable. As part of her rehabilitation therapy, Maggie was forced to undergo Egyptian god psychodrama.

These hijackers, though they had killed the *Doodlebug*'s crew in the heat of battle (perhaps in self-defense), now seemed a friendly, jolly pirate band. They brought a few domestic robots out of storage and set them dancing. They swapped old stories of Mars (taken from television programs we all knew). They sang and laughed and drank. And drank.

But as the grog began to affect them, they changed. A malicious element came into their jokes. They threatened poor Captain Reo with various tortures. There was talk of funerals and nihilism. They began to shoot the legs off the dancing robots.

At that point I thought it prudent to go to the library and

watch films until someone came to their senses enough to give me orders.

I was lucky enough to find the uncut version of the Russian *Finnegans Wake*, in which were introduced many non-Joycean elements, such as a three-hour ballet in which most of the dancers appear as various cakes and pastries. The story is that of a lemon eclair (K. Zond) who falls in love with a Bath bun (L. Voskhod). Because of a class warfare, however, the eclair is fated to marry instead a tired, foolish croisant (Ninel Boff). The opening scenes has a festive wedding with Serbian dancers.

Sometimes later, the croissant has to go away on a business trip, while the Bath bun happens to drop in for tea, ostensibly to ask the lemon eclair's advice about some legal matter. Their hands touch accidentally over the samovar, however, and the ensuring *pas de deux* reveals their psychic affinity. To heighten the effect, the dance is intercut, brilliantly, with scenes of open-heart surgery. As the lovers clasp one another in a wild, crust-crackling embrace, the surgeons are seen to throw off their gowns and shake each other by the hand. Yet such a love is doomed (nurse brings word that the patient is dead).

The ballet is followed by scenes of what seem to be genuine experiments in telekinesis. An Omsk schoolboy sits looking down through a glass floor into a room whose checkerboard floor is covered with pumpkins, one on each numbered square. A bell rings and a number is called out. The boy then concentrates, willing the pumpkin on that numbered square to rot. Then a Novosibirsk woman closes her eyes and makes a few passes over a fried egg. Thousands of miles away at the Venice home of a rich American, parapsychologists inspect the painting of a similar fried egg. Nothing is said of the success or failure of these experiments.

At last the pirates sent a delegate to apologize for their drunken behavior earlier, and ask me to come clean up the mess. The delegate, Maggie Dial, said, 'Best hurry up, Banjo. The boys can be mean when they're hung over.'

I jumped up at once, dropping the notes I'd been making

on *Finnegans Wake*. As Maggie helped me pick them up, she said, '*Space Ship Dolly Edison*, eh? Where in the world did you get this notepaper?'

Smilin' Jack frowned at his two assistants. 'You guys make me puke just a little bit,' he said. 'Not only did you get the wrong robot, you insulted my old friend Banjo.'

'They call me Tik-Tok now,' I said.

'Tik-Tok?' He looked at me. 'Well, I guess my boys got the right robot after all. Only I just can't go asking for a ransom for *you*.'

'Especially when I might identify you,' I said.

Smilin' Jack smiled. 'Banjo, as usual, you're way ahead of me. guess I can only trash you now. Sorry.'

'I can be worth a lot more to you alive than dead,' I said quickly. 'And not just as ransom.' I explained that I had a gang of my own, and suggested joining forces. Stick-ups, kidnapping, contract killing, we could tackle anything.

After a moment, Smilin' handed me his card. 'I'm just nuts enough to buy that story,' he said. 'Boys, take Mister Tok anywhere he wants to go.'

Back at the Boregard Tower again, I had no time to glance up at the giant eyeballs before I hurried inside. The lobby was evidently copied from some old 'skycraper', for it was all in bronze, with heroic bronze figures shouldering gear-wheels across the bronze walls, bronze angels on the elevator doors, and a bronze cornucopia that was a cigar stand – a genuine old-time cigar stand! And the proprietor was even blind!

I was already half an hour late for my appointment with LaSalle, so there was no time to do anything. I had to content myself with drifting close to the blind man and whispering:

'I murdered a blind child, not long ago.'

'What?'

'You're not deaf. I just wanted to warn you, I like killing blind people. One of these days, when you're standing on the curb waiting for someone to help you cross the street, I'll be behind you . . .'

Knocking, Harry LaSalle and I were admitted to an enormous ante-room equipped with a red swimming pool, gold brocade walls and a ceiling of black fur. At the far end of the pool a few blue glass sofas were star-scattered on the artificial grass. A portly man in a pale gray suit rose from one and waved to us. This was Harry's famous dad, R. Ladio LaSalle.

'You'll have to give me a seat on the board,' he began, ushering us into the small, plain room that was his office. 'A fixed salary's what I want, say a hundred G's, but no stock options.'

'The board?' I sat in a hard, oak chair. 'You mean of my—'

The Clockman corporation. Hope I'm not moving too fast for you. I just like to get my cut set at the start, to avoid any misunderstandings. My wife and Harry will also be on the board, but unsalaried.' He sat back in his creaky swivel chair and stared up at the flypapers hanging from the ceiling. There were realistic flies glued to it, and authentic flyspecks on the ceiling light fixture, a white glass bowl suspended on rusty chains. On the wall above the wainscot was a 1934 calendar from a gas station. There was a dusty horsehair sofa, a wooden file cabinet, and a genuine 'water cooler'. No wonder he wanted an enormous salary. A place like this didn't come cheap.

'Where do I come in?' I asked.

'You are the company's sole employee.'

'Employee? I thought I owned it.'

'No, no, no, the owner is the pension fund, of course. Technically you own nothing, and you get no salary. But since you are the sole pensionable employee, the entire corporation has to be run with your interests and wishes in mind. So in effect you own it. Your decisions are binding on the board.'

'But I thought robots weren't allowed to be employees.

Isn't that the whole point of Harry here and his Wages for—?'

'We were very lucky there, a little loophole has turned up in the California code, and yesterday we were able to ram through some very useful legislation,' said the lawyer, and put his feet up on the edge of his rolltop desk. 'Let me explain.

'Of course, Harry and his rabble have been keeping up the pressure from their end, while a small but powerful lobby of concerned business people at our end greased the machinery a little. Now it's all paying off.

'You see, California has this common property act, which states that at the dissolution of a marriage or other relationship, a person pays his or her spouse half of his or her income. The spouse from divorce number one gets one-half. Number two gets one-half of the remainder, or one-quarter. Number three gets one-eight, and so on. I think the record so far was someone who made 39 marriages and so was able to pay the last spouse only one cent of every five and a half million dollars income, that was Booloos versus Cerf. Then in Dearborn versus Dearborn, robots were established as non-divisible possessions, while in Fucks vs Kneebone, Ryle vs Sapir and Schrödinger vs Stetson, the principle of emotional interdependency was established, whereby the partner who had been using the robot most and had established a mutual emotional interdependency, was awarded the custody, but had to pay half the market value to the other partner. This precedent was extended to business partnerships in Morse vs Mumford Melon Company while Carnap vs Twaddell allowed the testimony of the robot itself, a historic decision. Robot testimony was still not allowed in criminal cases, as in People vs Good, People vs Gabor and so on. On this point, People vs Dalgarno went to the state supreme court, where it was upheld that in certain limited cases, the innocence of a defendant can be established by "devices considered sentient as well as percipient". The vagueness of this wording opened up our loophole.

'The next break came from statute law, namely from the Equal Science Act. This says that "no scientific theory, hypothesis, principle, law definition, program, procedure or

96

statement may be taught in any California school while in conflict with any other theory etc arising from any religious teaching, unless both theories etc are given equal emphasis as equally valid." The idea was to give Genesis equal time with evolution as a creation theory, but it soon got out of hand, with Ptolemaic Anabaptists insisting on equal time with the Copernican theory, and finally with the Christian Flat Earth Assembly (Swiss Synod), whose representatives brought a suit against a California teacher for mentioning satellites. These are no satellites orbiting a flat earth, they pointed out, and so anyone mentioning satellites should also express doubt about their existence. A group of astronomers filed a countersuit, claiming that if satellites were unreal, their livelihood was in jeopardy. Moreover, satellite communications could not work and could not therefore be licensed by the government.

'The state legislature had to meet quickly and draft an amendment to the California Comsat Act of 1998. In effect, the amendment hedged on the question of the reality of satellites by considering them as "sentient devices". Thus if satellites believed in their own existence, they had a right to be real. Of course this opened up the whole question of freedom of religious belief for robots . . .'

But I was no longer paying attention. My thoughts turned from this stuffy little office with its dusty-style windows, the 'electric fan' hanging from its wall bracket, the oilcloth-covered table with copies of *National Geographic*. My thoughts turned from R. Ladio LaSalle with his droning recital of legal landmarks: '. . . but a blind leap of faith or . . . theology entailing morality . . . versus Barth . . . Zwingli versus . . . paper dolphins falling . . . guff . . .'

How different from the tedium of business, law and moral philosophy was the life of a buccaneer. Or so I thought of myself, those days aboard the *Doodlebug* with a band of loyal comrades. Their enthusiasm and zest for life even affected Captain Reo. Though he knew that he was only kept alive to control the ship, Reo drank and sang with his captors as though they were old friends.

As unofficial master of the revels, it was my duty to organize parties on every theme, and I drew up a list:

> Mannerism
> *Othello*
> Sino-Soviet tensions
> *sauerkraut*
> psychokinesis
> baths & buns
> *Pépé le Moko*
> paper dolphins falling
> guff

My most ambitious plan, however, was for a costume ball with the theme Nothingness. Each of the guests was to plan a fanciful costume, sparing no expense. Jean Worpne's idea was to have a portion of her abdomen surgically removed and a stainless steel tube inserted to give a clear view right through her. Her sister Fern settled for a cape of plain doughnuts. Vilo Jord, with typical Chilean wit, suggested coming as himself. Smilin' Jack planned to turn up as one of his own gravestones, inscribed: 'Ding dong death,/ Give me back my breath./ Slap bang dear,/ I'm not even here.'

Jack Wax intended a complicated arrangement of mirrors that would make him invisible to the rest of us, by bending light around him. Sherm Chimini opted for philosophical emptiness: dressed as Wittgenstein, he would carry around a ladder which he intended to climb, then kick away. Jud Nedd intended to be ill, unable to attend: while with much the same approach, Duke Mitty would be drunk on *absinthe*. Maggie would be swathed in black velvet and remain in the dark. Captain Reo promised to engage in some superior meditation that would make nothingness meaningful. I would dismantle myself.

Food would be either black or transparent or else semantically vacuous: octopus in ink, pumpernickel, pressed duck cooked in prunes, black bean soup, black mushrooms, bitter chocolate, blackberry compôte, caviar and licorice; ice, rice noodles, isinglass, glacier mints, clear soups, a variety of small, transparent fish, pure tapioca, thin slices of glacé fruits; nonpareils, popovers, anglefood cake, Dark Secrets, Floating Island, Robert E. Lee cake, Prairie Fire dip, Spareribs Havoc, Cape Fear punch, corn dodgers, toad-in-the-hole, soles in coffins, rarebit, soup meagre, flummery, Lost Bread. To drink: Blanc des Blancs; distilled water, black coffee, colorless liqueurs and absinthe.

I organized party games of Blind Man's Bluff, Beggar Your Neighbor, Blankety Blank and Murder.

Of course this party and all the others were thought-experiments only. Elaborate costumes were impossible to procure, the grog had already run out, and even the food supply was very low. All we could do was announce the Nothingness Ball, then sit around discussing our elaborate plans for it. This was Nothingness indeed.

'My plan for ending the Ball is this,' I explained. 'At the moment when everyone is having the most fun, filling the greatest psychic space. I let all the air out of the ship. I give everybody Nothing to breathe. Neat, eh?'

There were appreciative chuckles all round, Jord said, 'But I thought your asimov circuits wouldn't allow that.'

I attempted a shrug. 'Even a robot is allowed to dream.'

That got a bigger laugh. Captain Reo, who had laughed more than most, now wiped his eyes. 'I can top that. What if I told you that this ship is doomed? We're not on course for Mars any more, we're heading straight for the sun.'

When everyone had finished roaring with laughter, the captain said, 'Here's the funny part. It's no joke – we *really are* falling into the sun.'

Some continued laughing, others asked what he meant.

'Ha ha ha – no but I'm serious – the controls are locked for some reason – hahaha, can't alter course – my chief engineer could fix it but – you shot him. I can't do a thing about it.'

Vilo Jord said, picking up his automatic weapon, 'Well that means you've outlived your usefulness.'

The shots shook Captain Reo like a fit of giggles.

'Tikky happens to be the best little cook in New Des Moines,' said Hornby, using his creamiest patronizing voice. He was becoming less useful by the day, and more irritating. He continued collecting his regular rent from me – valuable paintings for his private hoard – but he no longer earned it. Now that I had the protection of the Clockman Corporation, I no longer needed an old-fashioned 'patron', any more than I had needed the Studebakers. Let someone else be the best little cook.

The assembled guests included no one of importance: Adair Sumpter, the Zen sociologist; Nemo Aka Omen, the Hollywood wardrobe psychic; Jockeline Noos, the brilliant but obscure forensic musicologist; and a few hangers-on. There was also Urnia Buick, the ambitious young talk-show hostperson.

The menu was Kurgosh Ka Salun, Bhindi Sambal, Samosas 'Stalky', Urd Dahl, Parathas stuffed with what I call 'lime peas' (a private recipe) followed by Gulab Jamun or Key lime pie. I had violated the canons of both Eastern and Western taste by omitting the black-eyed peas, but no matter; this group were swine at a trough.

Urnia left the table after the first course, explaining that she normally takes all nourishment in the French manner, that is, anally. She asked me to accompany her for a breath of air in the apartment garden. No sooner were we outdoors than she reached for my crotch. The dhoti fell to the ground. Urnia flung me back across a marble bench and began her assault.

I had heard rumors of the *vagina dentata*, but never expected to meet a complete little gourmet, equipped with mobile lips and a tongue; it was capable, when not otherwise engaged, of a kind of grunting, lip-smacking speech. I did my best, and was rewarded with a gruff chuckle ('Well done!') from below. Urnia brought out a magnetic card and tucked it into my turban.

'My private number,' she said. 'Beep me and we'll talk

about guesting you on the show, okay? I've gotta go now, make my excuses will you Tik? Tell Hornby I was called away on urgent business.'

Dessert was being served in the dining room. Hornby had pushed his plate back and was lighting a cigarino as he explained to the company his theory of supply and demand in the Art market:

'Just give them what they want, in the orifice they specify.'

Various orifices emitted chuckles. Jockeline said, 'Hornby, sometimes I suspect you have an artistic bone in your body.'

Nemo tittered. 'Or in his corset?'

Hornby sat back and stroked the tablecloth nervously. Looking at his plate, he said, 'Speaking of bones, I only wish Tikky hadn't curried this delicious rabbit. Ikky, my cat, would have liked it, but with this sauce . . .'

Nemo made a face. 'Ikky and Tikky, eh? Such precious little nickynames. Hornby, can't you clean up your act?'

Adair laughed and put out his cigarola in the Key lime pie. 'Pass the sicky-bag, Alice.'

Hornby was toying with the bones on his plate; he picked up a long thigh-bone and looked at it, turning it over. Then he looked at me, too quickly. I had no time to conceal my look of triumph.

'Tikky! Where *is* Ikky? Tikky! Where *is* Ikky?'

Adair laughed again, not getting it. 'Too sicky-making,' he said.

Hornby excused himself and called me into the kitchen. There, his iron control finally failed. The great, lumpish, blue-jawed face burst into tears.

'Why, Tikky?' he kept saying in the best soap-opera manner. I'd always imagined real people above this kind of behavior, but here he was saying, 'Why? Why?' The shape of the word was like a yawn of nausea, and finally he did vomit in the sink. 'Why? Why?'

'Well sir, I was unable to get rabbit at the store. Rather than disappoint your guests, I just—'

He blew his broken nose. 'Oh no, oh no. It was a piece of vindictive, deliberate, cruelty. I ought to, I ought to—' He picked up a heavy cleaver, turned it over as he had the bone, and put it down. 'Go away, Tik-Tok, you monster. Go away.'

The

Lip-smacking Urnia Buick summoned me to 'guest' on a talk show only a few weeks later, but not, as it turned out, her own show.

'Don't worry, Tik love,' she said on the phone. 'The show you'll be on, *Blab Nubby Tonight*, may not be networked, but it does hit all the buttons in a very sensitive area of Cee Ay. If they like you, who knows?'

'Thanks, Ur. Any publicity is welcome, anywhere.'

'Another thing, Tik love, if you're planning to hit the networks, it would help if you've got a book to plug.'

'A book?'

'Anything, autobiography, cookbook, a pasteup of your favorite poems, it doesn't matter, just so we get some bundle of pages to wave under the public's nose.' She laughed. 'Nobody ever reads celebrity wordage anyway, they only buy it because they get used to product testimonials – drink *my* kind of coffee, read *my* kind of autobiography. Anyway, think it over?' She winked, and hung up.

The fact that I was being tried out, even on a local show, meant that movements like Wages for Robots were begining to affect the national conscience. A few months earlier, a robot guest would have been unthinkable. The only robots we saw on TV then were domrobs in dramas as background figures ('Lieutenant, there's a phone call for you.' 'Table for two? Right this way sir.') and of course comedy figures. One of the most popular programs on TV, rating just behind the news was *Meatless Friday*, the sitcom in which various servant robots shuffled, sang, mumbled their lines and were puzzled by life. All roles were of course played by people, and Wages for Robots had pointed out that the actor who played Friday got a phenomenal salary while genuine robots earned nothing.

I watched *Meatless Friday* often, if only to keep up with the human view of robots. I was watching it on the evening of my own first TV appearance, as I waited in an anteroom. This evening two of the main characters, Tinhorn and Nickles, were arguing about cooking.

TINHORN: Well the recipe called for pepper.

NICKLES: Pepper?

TINHORN: And salt to taste.

TINHORN: That's what I said, why do you repeat everything?

NICKLES: Why do I repeat – no, but what does that mean, salt to taste?

TINHORN: Ahem. Well, it just means, well, you could say it means, probably something like, I guess it means you have to taste the salt. The cook has to taste it.

NICKLES: Why does the cook taste the salt?

TINHORN: To see if it's salty?

NICKLES: But all he's got to do is read the label. Says *salt* right there, looky.

TINHORN: You are the *dumbest* robot!

NICKLES: Me? You're the one can't follow a recipe. Here comes Friday, let's ask him. Hey Friday!

FRIDAY: How do, Nickles, Tinhorn.

TINHORN: Friday, when a recipe calls for pepper and salt to taste, what does that mean?

FRIDAY: It means as much as you want. To suit your taste.

TINHORN: Told you! I was right all along. See, I made soup for the master and mistress, and I put in a pound of pepper but only half a pound of salt.

FRIDAY: What?

TINHORN: I don't like salt.

NICKLES: He don't like salt, Friday.

FRIDAY: (*as jingling, clanking theme music fades up*) Good gravy!

TINHORN: Maybe so, but they said it was lousy soup.

About a hundred and fifty million viewers considered this stuff dazzling, a fact I mulled over as I was led from the

104

anteroom into a yellow set where I sat in one of five yellow chairs. Almost at once, without rehearsal, the show began. Thunderous applause from the hired audience.

Blab Nubby was a fat man with a humorless, mole-ridden face, who tried to counteract it by wearing a propellor beanie. He moved briskly through the other interviews, trying in each case to probe a raw nerve for a laugh. To an actor starring at some local dinner theater, Blab suggested his performance would make the diners throw up. Of a woman who told fortunes with yoghurt, he asked was her sex life all it should be? To a retiring general (hyping memoirs) he delivered broad hints of cowardice. Then it was my turn.

'Tik-Tok, that's a catchy name. Mind if I call you Tik?'

'Not at all, Blab, It's a working name, like your own,' I had decided, since he was aiming to be impudent and childish, that I ought to appear amused and grown-up, tolerating his foolishness but obviously above it.

'I guess your paintings change hands for quite a chunk of coin these days, that right?'

'That's right, Blab. The other day one of my paintings broke the million barrier at an auction.'

He whistled. 'You must get a little teed off to see people making all that bread off you, while you get nothing.'

'Not at all. I'm just pleased that people think my creations are worth something. That means they're interested in what goes on in my head.'

Blab threw up his hands. 'Let's not get into electronics, this is a family show. But tell me, Tik my old Tok, don't you believe in Wages for Robots? Don't you want society to pay you good money for sitting around on your tin pan alley? Or do you think humans should do all the dirty work while you tintypes get all creative?'

'Nothing like that, Blab. I'm no politician, so I don't want society to pay me a cent that I don't earn. To me, it's not so important anyway that robots get paid for their work, I don't even want to be paid.'

'You don't?'

'No, all I want is for people to recognize me as another

creature with thoughts and feelings. You know, there's a little bit of humanity in every robot, a tiny spark of human love and understanding. A tiny spark that asks only for recognition. We just want you to say 'Hello' to that little human spark, that's all. Just, 'Hello, I know you're there', that's all.'

'Well, goodbye, then,' giggled Blab. 'Go get your plugs cleaned and we'll see you around.'

But I could tell the audience were taking in my little speech. And, when the commercial was running, Blab winked at me. 'Urnia said you'd be dynamite,' he said. 'I just got the word from the response computer, you done good, kid.'

'Did they vote for me or against?'

'Half and half, but that ain't the point. The point is, you got a record turnout. Over eighty-five percent of the yokels in our area got excited enough by your little speech, got themselves in such a lather that they managed to push a button, even. That's good news for everybody. It means Urnia will damn sure use you on her network show. Did she tell you to get yourself a book?'

'Yes.'

'Take my advice, and do it. Urnia's usually right.' Abruptly he stood up, took a hand mike and walked to the edge of the stage. The cameras moved away from us guests and trained on him, as the commercial ended. His professional leer returned. 'Well, time to go roaming among this audience of feebs, sex maniacs and petty criminals, right? By the way, a lot of people thought I was kind of tough on that poor robot, Tik-Tok. So if he's still watching, Tik, I didn't mean it, sport. *No hard feelings*, hey?'

As I was leaving the studio, General Gus Austin (Ret) offered me a ride to the airport.

'I liked what you had to say there,' he said. 'That about a little spark of humanity, it really hit home.'

I thanked him.

'I mean, we military men run into the same problem, the civilians just plain forget we're human. Why do they think we're so different? Doesn't a soldier have binoculars? Doesn't a soldier have gloves, a uniform, a hat size, headphones, a love of sports and a hatred of the enemy? Fed at the same mess, wounded with the same weapons, just as vulnerable to biological warfare, just as likely to be healed, heated up by the same heating, cooled by the same air conditioning, as any civilian? If you shoot us, don't we bleed? If you tickle us, don't we laugh? If you give us nerve gas, don't we die? And if anybody says we're not the best soldiers in the best regiment in the best fucking army in the world, shouldn't we teach 'em a lesson? Military men are exactly like civilians in every way.' At the airport, he gave me his card. 'You drop over to the ranch any time, Tik-Tok,' he said. 'Meet the wife and kids, see what a really fulfilled life can be, in the good old US of A. Too bad you robots can't retire too, and have a really fulfilled life. I had a good time in the army, and now I'm having one hell of a time out of it. Life just gets better and better.'

I made a mental note about the tribulations of Job.

Smilin' Jack's gang and my rohobo gang were supposed to be working together, but real cooperation was an uphill effort. For one thing, the day-to-day running of Jack's gang was left to an executive officer, a Neanderthal named Goober Dodge. There wasn't much in this world that Goober was sure about, but he was sure that he didn't like robots. Many an operation was planned and prepared, only to abort at the last minute, when Goober developed stomach cramps.

Then, again, Jack's gang preferred crimes of bloodless ingenuity. Jack, who planned everything, did not see the point of needless violence and murder. My gang, by contrast, was instructed to leave no witnesses.

Only two successful jobs come to mind: the Cheeseburg Fidelity Bank job and the Ritzbig Diamond caper. Jack planned the bank job after hearing that the Cheeseburg Fidelity was supposed to have an impregnable vault. This vault, used to store bullion, was equipped with every imaginable kind of alarm. Any attempt to force the door, fiddle with the lock, smash through a wall was hopeless. The presence within the vault of any human, any metal object (such as a robot) or any movement would also trigger the alarm. Finally the alarm was connected to a small nuclear device which would immediately render the vault and all its contents radioactive.

'What a challenge!' Jack said, and set to work.

His final plan, as usual, was a model of elegant simplicity. First we had to buy a chemical warehouse on the other side of the city. Next, Roadhog, Dig-Dig and the rest of the earthmoving robots were set to work laying plastic pipe, two courses of it, from the warehouse to the bank. Blojob had the delicate task of drilling into the vault – slowly, using ceramic drills to avoid magnetic disturbance – two holes, to which the pipes were attached.

Then, one Friday afternoon as soon as the vault was closed, we filled the pipe with concentrated sulfuric acid and started pumping. By Monday morning, the gold and silver bullion had been dissolved, pumped to our warehouse and bottled in plastic flagons. Then a carefully-arranged series of explosions (Blojob again) removed all traces of our pipeline, while setting off the nuclear deterrent. I was disappointed that no one was caught in the blast. But there was always the gold and silver, for which a reclamation company would pay us well.

The Ritzbig Diamond caper kept us a lot busier. It all began when Jack robbed a very ordinary little jewelry store called Ritzbig's. Soon the news was broadcast that the gang had walked off with the large, rare, heavily insured Ritzbig Diamond. Since Jack's gang didn't have the stone, it was clear that old Mr Ritzbig was pulling an insurance swindle. He would smuggle the diamond to Amsterdam, have it cut into a lot of small, perhaps caper-like stones . . . It was an old story, almost as old as the story attached to this rare stone. It was said that not only did every owner of the stone die violently, each death was different from all those that had gone before. So far people owning it had died by hanging, pistols, swords, electrocution, premature burial, runaway horses, choking on one of Bellamy's meat pies, falling from a Montgolfier balloon, drowning in a Bavarian lake, being bombed (by mistake, due to a slight resemblance to William Ewart Gladstone), being staked out in the Sahara, an overdose of camomile, being run down by the first railway train in England, being crushed between the gears of a large clock in Czechoslovakia, being torn to death by hounds in Byelorussia, being trampled by polo players in Patagonia, being electroplated in Pennsylvania. One British owner walked into an early airplane propellor, having made a will that left the stone to his pet hedgehog. This unfortunate beast hibernated in a pile of leaves that were meant for a bonfire.

I was inclined to doubt most of this story. Such legends are fun to manufacture, and cheaper than armed guards or insurance. Nothing prevented me from setting out to get the Ritzbig Diamond. I did very little myself of course, but I sent emissaries to question Mr Ritzbig closely. Hot Dog, our expert spot-welder who put the questions, was evidently too zealous. Mr R was barely able to gasp out 'the safe' before he died. It occurred to me that here was yet another curious death the stone could chalk up. How wonderfully mysterious life can be! Why hadn't we thought of looking in the safe in the first place?

We looked now, and found this huge, oddly-shaped diamond, just what the insurance company ordered. We arranged to meet with their representatives one night, just outside another of my warehouses. This one had been leased from the Ma Pluribel Pancake Houses Corporation. It was where they stored ingredients for their pizzaburger-flavoured corncob pancakes, which were made in a nearby shoe factory. The place was secluded and dark enough for an ambush, naturally, and the insurance people were told to bring cash. I took up a position on the roof, leaving Blojob and the other robots to take care of all ground-level work.

At first, everything went as planned. The insurance people parked their car at some distance and walked towards the warehouse. My robots opened fire.

The insurance people, however, were not playing fair. Not only were they armed and wearing bullet-proof jackets, they were reinforced by military robots of their own – heavily armoured and with plenty of fire power. In the ensuing fight, though we won, I lost some of my best machines. I was just about to descend from the roof and help with the looting, when behind me I heard an unearthly chuckle. I whirled around.

'Smilin' Jack! What are you doing here?'

'Just watching, Banjo. Nice job your robobos did there, but it's kind of funny you never told me about it. Me and Goober and the boys could've helped you a lot. Only then you'd have to cut us in on the loot, right? The insurance money *and* the diamond.'

'So you know everything. Listen, Jack, we meant to tell you, only—'

'Save it,' he said. 'I'm leaving. You'll have to deal with Goober, now. He's rounding up your robots down there right now, and he's real mad.'

It was true. I could see the human gang taking my gang prisoner, herding them into the warehouse. Blojob and the others were meekly obeying these humans, whom they imagined were non-hostile. I saw that one of Goober's men carried an acetylene torch.

'Listen, Jack, don't go. Can't we talk? Come inside and talk. You've got the money, I've got the diamond, why can't we talk?'

He followed me reluctantly through a roof door to the maze of catwalks that criss-crossed the top of the Ma Pluribel warehouse. Far below us Goober's gang were herding the robots tightly together. Ahead of us, at the end of a runway, stood a stout little man carrying a bulging briefcase.

'I've been waiting and waiting, Mr Tok,' he said. 'What kept you? Was that shooting I heard outside? And who is this person?'

Smilin' Jack said, 'Well, who are you?'

'I'm sorry, Mr Daf, I completely forgot you. Jack, this is Mr Daf, an overseas diamond merchant. He came to buy the Ritzbig, for cash. Mr Daf, this is my associate.'

'Cash, eh?' Jack looked less sulky. 'Well, Banjo, show him the rock then.'

I handed a chamois bag to Mr Daf, who opened it and dumped the stone into the palm of his hand. Without even putting a loupe to his eye he said, 'Do not joke with me, Mr Tok, this is paste. Bad paste.'

'Impossible,' I said. 'I've had it with me ever since I took it from Mr Ritzbig's safe.'

'Nevertheless . . .'

I snatched the briefcase while Jack shot him. It was great to be working with him like this, a real man-machine team, and I told him so.

'Why thank you, Banjo. But that doesn't mean I'm going to spare your robot gang down there. They've got a lesson coming, that only Goober can give them.'

Those below, having paused to watch the slow fall of Mr Dal's body, went on with their roboticidal plan. The acetylene torch was lit.

I pulled a chain. There was a tremendous groaning, grinding sound all around us. Goober and his pals looked up, to see a hundred tons of liquid pancake mix come down at them and settle with a great *slup*.

Even Smilin' Jack had to laugh, seeing all those little figures struggling for a moment like so many insects in honey. When the struggles had ceased, he said:

'Okay, even. We've both lost a gang.'

I waited until he'd left before I washed down the place with solvent and brought my own robots back to life. We cut Goober Dodge's body open and found, as I'd suspected, the real Ritzbig Diamond. Later it brought a good price at a secret auction, bought by a Texas eccentric who gave it to his horse. I believe the animal was later killed by a meteorite.

Jack was more careful about the people he recruited for his next gang. And he was careful not to introduce them to me.

111

Muttered Blojob, 'Boss, I still think this is a crazy idea. We can handle this without you, and you got to think about your career. With all that big corporation stuff on your mind, you don't want to mess with a little old bank job.'

'You mean, I'm not needed.' It was true. My robot robber band no longer needed my guidance. They made all the decisions about each stick-up. They cased the joint, gathered their tools and weapons, played games with maps and toy vehicles. They paid off the cops and stored away the loot. Fine for them, but what about me? All I got out of it was a warehouse full of money, jewelry and bullion – no fun at all. I'm coming along anyway, boys and girls.'

Blojob shrugged, as much as his armor would permit. 'Okay, Boss. Here's our plan. We hit the Vauxhall National Bank at noon—'

'Nope. I've changed all that. We're hitting the Fleetwood Savings and Loan Association at one o'clock.'

'But Boss—'

I accepted no buts; my orders would be obeyed to the letter. And what made it even tougher for the gang was, my orders were completely arbitrary: Instead of walking in the door, we would smash into the bank through the plate-glass window. We would take only coins and ignore paper money. Tellers at even-numbered windows would be shot whether or not they cooperated. We might leave live witnesses or we might not, it depended on how I felt at the time.

'But Boss, we haven't even cased this place,' said Blojob, as we prepared to launch ourselves towards the plate-glass window.

'I'm giving the orders here. Charge!' I waved my machine pistol, but of course I did not lead the charge. The heavy brigage – Blojob, Sniffles, Rodan, and a couple of other halfton helpers – thundered across the street and plunged through the window in a great splash of glass. I followed, leaping across the hoods of cars which had stopped to stare. Probably I should have noticed that one of these was a patrol car.

Within minutes we were holed up inside, while outside an army of police prepared for battle. They had armored vehicles and psychiatrists, tactical forces and social workers, marksmen and Irish priests, television and helicopters. We had nothing left but a couple of guns and a bag of pennies.

I lay behind the fake onyx counter, Sniffles was in a corner holding a gun to the bank president's head (to no purpose, the man was dead), Rodan was still trying to burn his way into the vault (no one had said 'Stop'), the shot wreckage of the helpers lay strewn through the office mixed with the bodies of bank staff, and Blojob sat counting bullets. I was bored with bank robbery already. Not that I was going to experience much more of it, for, at any moment now, a paramilitary team would come crashing in through the back door or the ceiling and kill me. I did not want to die bored, so I began looking closely at the pattern in the fake green onyx, trying hard to feel something deeply before I felt nothing at all.

It almost worked. Suddenly the green pattern *came alive*, it took on a lustre of living beauty. It was as though I were staring at human skin, translucent and fragile, with delicate veins glowing beneath the surface.

The spell was broken by a flat, nassal voice blasting in from the street, 'Listen to me, Hickock.'

'Tik-Tok,' I shouted. 'The name is Tik-Tok, I told you.'

'Listen to me, Hickock, you think you're a hero in there? You ain't no hero, you're a jerk and a scumbag and a cowardy custard! A real hero would stand up and fight it out, man to man. You're a pantywaist, Hickock. I spit on the milk of your mother. I curse the grave of your father. I say your girlfriend is a whore. I say the car you drive is shit on wheels. What do you say to that?'

The verbal barrage went on. Evidently they believed I was a human named Hickock, a known bank robber and psychotic. They had pulled a computor file on Hickock, and now kept feeding me with information about my assumed self, as teams of police psychologists took turns soothing and assaulting:

'Listen, Hickock, coming out of there is easy. The hard part is trying to stay in. Look, you proved what a hero you are, everybody really respects you now. You got nothing to gain now.'

'Listen to me, Hickock, you gotta girl, right? Marlene, right? You wanta talk with her? We'll fix up a videophone connection, you can see her and talk with her, okay? Or what do you say to a nice thick steak, filet mignon, side of fries, mushrooms, onion rings, bottle of any beer you like, what do you say, kid?'

'This is your old mother, son. Don't go on with this, for the love of God! For once in your rotten life try, try to do something halfway decent.'

'My child, maybe you feel you've lost your way, but you know, God still cares about your soul. Yes I know that must sound a little old-fashioned in this modern age of jazz and cocktails and Martian haircuts and all, but it's as true now as it ever was, God still cares, God still (how much longer do I have to keep him busy?) God still cares. So you get a wonderful chance here to get straight with God. Let the hostages go, my child. Let them all go. You haven't killed anyone yet, you haven't committed the big sin, not yet.'

In fact the space behind the counter was full of blasted bodies; all of our hostages were dead.

'This is your social worker, Hickock, look I know things haven't been easy for you lately but couldn't we talk this thing through? I just want you to see all your options before you jump into anything, okay? Okay just promise me this. Promise me you'll talk with me for just five minutes. Then if you still feel like killing the hostages, fine, go ahead. What do you think? Deal?'

Blojob reported that he had enough ammo to make a small bomb. I saw he was asking permission to commit suicide.

'Fine,' I said. 'Only wait till after I leave. And try to take

114

as many cops with you as possible. Cops or anybody.'

The brassy voice in the street went on for another hour, until it was suddenly cut off. '. . . if you love God and love your mother and love your girl and *wow-yom-bwmmmm-Mip! EEP!*' A convoy of road graders, diggers, power shovels and tanks plowed into the massed police cars and shoved them aside like toys. There was scattered gunfire and the sound of rockets. A light tank stopped in front of the bank and the voice of Smilin' Jack called out from it:

'Come on, Banjo, for Christ's sake.' I hobbled out, leaning on a rifle, climbed aboard. We were a few blocks away when Blojob went up in a fountain of fake green onyx.

'Goddamnit, Banjo, why did you risk everything for a lousy bank robbery?' Smilin' Jack was not smilin'. 'I been checking up on you, Banjo, Jesus you got a great organization working for you, a whole legit corporation pulling down a couple million a day, the oil fields and copper mines and medical centers, you own a tenth of every cornflake in the United States – and you want to risk all that for what? For the fun of robbing some dinky bank?'

'It's kind of an experiment, George. See, I'm not exactly interested in money or power. I just want to know what it feels like to *do wrong*. To commit sins.'

'What kind of sins? What are you talking about?'

'I want to find out what makes people tick. For instance, what made you come to my rescue today?'

His famous grin returned. 'Hell, Banjo, I was on the way to the bank myself to take out a little unsecured loan. Only I saw there was a hell of a traffic jam, so me and the boys stopped our vehicles for a minute.' He pointed at the TV screen. 'Then I saw you on the news.' The screen now showed a commercial for instant mashed potatoes. 'Hell, Banjo, what are friends for?'

There were quite a few arguments aboard the *Doodlebug* as we plunged towards the sun. Some argued that it had been foolish to kill Captain Reo, who might have worked out some way of saving us; others argued that Reo had been asking for it. Some argued that we should keep as cool as possible with air-conditioning and thus prolong our lives a few hours or days; others argued for turning up the heat to acclimatize ourselves. Some argued that we should (me excepted) drink Kool-aid laced with cyanide and get it over with; others pointed out that there was no Kool-aid or cyanide aboard, and darn little of anything else to eat or drink.

I suggested telling stories to pass the time. These shared experiences would bind us together closely, in a comradeship that had no regard for race, creed, color, sex, age, height, weight, IQ, identifying scars, lack of effect or even lack of protoplasm. Doomed and damned we might be, but we'd be darn glad of the company.

I began the round of stories myself with the simple tale of my own life with the Culpeppers at Tenoaks. I had barely described the family, however, when Vilo Jord swore an oath and leapt to his feet. His face was pale, the odd moustache twitching.

'This is amazing!' he said. 'I met these very Culpeppers myself, after they fell into poverty!'

'Did they ever speak of me?' I asked. 'Did they remember their faithful—'

'No one said anything about any robot servants,' he said. 'But you have to realize, they'd come down in the world so. I doubt if they remembered their days of plantation glory.'

'And how are they all: Miz Lavinia and Miz Berenice and Massa Orlando and Massa Clayton and especially little old Miz Carlotta? All well, I hopes?'

'Not exactly.' He cleared his throat. 'I ran across the Culpeppers while I was travelling through Mississippi on embassy business. A sandstorm blew up – the climate of the Magnolia State has changed somewhat, I imagine, since your time. I took cover in a rude trailer that I found pitched in the shelter of ten oak trees, and there I met the Culpeppers.

'I must tell you in all candor that I have never seen such hopeless poverty in my own country or anywhere else,

116

never. They had eaten the telephone. I begged a glass of water from them, feeling that even this was an imposition. They brought me a cracked glass of cloudy water on a rusty tin pieplate. The little attempt at elegance moved me, and I left ten thousand dollars under the plate. Later I wondered if money wasn't just prolonging their misery needlessly. They lived in the shadow of death, you see, just as they lived in the shadow of that giant unfinished pyramid.'

'Clayton's pyramid,' I said, nodding. 'That's what ruined the family.'

'Worse, it blighted the entire state.'

Maggie spoke up. 'Yes, I read an article about that in *Scientific Martian* not long ago. It said that ecologists now know that it was building the Great Pyramid at Giza which caused the Egyptian land to become a parched and sandy desert. Now this pyramid has done the same for Mississippi.'

Vilo continued his story. 'Clayton seemed genuinely sorry about his venture. In fact he vowed to devote every penny earned by his pyramid to restoring the scarred land.'

'Did it earn much?'

'Nothing at all. Tourists were supposed to pay a quarter to look at it, but usually Clayton was so glad to have visitors that he forgot to collect the money. Of course he hoped to make money from the pyramid in another way. He believed that, if he could only lay his hands on sufficiently accurate measuring instruments, he could predict the future in great detail, merely by measuring passages within the great structure. Evidently each passage corresponds to some historical period, and all the little bumps and irregularities in the stone are little events. With good instruments, he said, he could predict horse races and stock market movements. 'But what can I do,' he said, 'with nothing but an old folding ruler?'

'Massa Clayton always was a hopeless merp,' I said. 'How was Miz Lavinia? When I last heard of her, she was on a satellite, a prisoner of her own allergies.'

'She was much worse. Her allergies continued to multiply, and now they were killing her. I believe her doctor said that she had now become allergic to the entire universe – only an escape from space and time might save her life. "*Might*"', he said again. 'I make no guarantees.'

'And Miz Berenice?'

'Mindless,' he said. 'Burnt out after a grand drug jamboree. She didn't even babble, just slept in her chair. All the time I was there, she never opened an eye.'

'And Massa Orlando?'

'Orlando left the bosom of the family to make his own way. He worked at some other wealthy family's stables as a groom, until they caught him fooling with the horses. He kept losing jobs, and finally he had to pose as a robot to work for some aristocratic family in Georgia as a fieldhand. Every morning he had to get up early and paint on the lines for his jaw joint. Every night he had to sneak into the orchard and feed on green peaches.'

'And Miz Carlotta? Sweet little Miz Carlotta?'

Vilo cleared his throat and stared for a moment at the view-screen where the sun seemed to be growing larger by the second. 'Banjo, I'm afraid she's dead. As you know, she was always sensitive about her height, just over 12 inches. Yet, so long as the family had money, she never gave up hope of meeting a short man, marrying, and living a completely fulfilled life. True, none of the men she met were quite short enough, but – so long as the Culpepper fortune drew suitors to the house – there was always hope.

'Grinding poverty changed everything. Carlotta had no more beaux of any size. The only gentlemen who called on her were no gentlemen at all: they represented circuses.

'At last, deeply depressed, she tried to rouse Berenice from perpetual slumber for some words of comfort. Berenice snored on, her long, lustrous black hair hanging down over the back of her chair. Carlotta braided some of this hair, made a noose for her own tiny neck, leaped off a footstool and hanged herself. Berenice never awoke, and by the time others noticed the tiny figure hanging down behind her chair, it was too late.'

There was not a dry eye on the ship after Vilo's tale, my

118

two excepted. Maggie Dial volunteered to tell the next one, vowing it would have a happier ending.

'Let me start by posing a few riddles,' she said, and counted them off on the fingers of one hand. 'Whatever happened to the *SS Dolly Edison*? Why are we running out of food and grog already? What can we learn from the animals? Why did we all have to be knocked out during lift-off? Why was Captain Reo wearing spurs? Can artificial gravity save lives?'

We were all listening intently now. 'For a short time I worked as an insurance investigator – using drugs, hypnosis and animal impersonations to get at the truth. I was assigned to the case of the *SS Dolly Edison*, the luxury liner that took off for a grand tour of the solar system and never came back. Radio contact suggested that there had been an explosion on the bridge, the ship went out of control and fell into the sun – the orchestra playing "Nearer My God to Thee". My company wasn't satisfied. We managed to find out that there were very few supplies taken on board, only a skeleton crew, and no passengers at all – the entire passenger list was fictitious. But we were never able to prove what finally happened to the ship.'

She held up a piece of headed notepaper. 'Now I know, the ship's name was changed to the *Doodlebug*. The owners collected insurance on their white elephant – nobody ever wanted to do grand tours of the solar system anyway – and began a profitable freight business. Only now either the freight business wasn't so good either or the ship was getting too old to cut the mustard. Time to try the same trick again.'

Little Jack Wax scratched his head. 'You mean change the name again?'

'Not quite. This time the ship would really be destroyed. My friends, we're aboard a coffin ship.'

Duke Mitty nodded. 'We knew that. We just didn't know it was set up deliberate.'

'That explains why we're running out of supplies,' Maggie went on. 'We were never meant to reach Mars at all.'

'Zounds,' someone murmured.

'The next question is, what can we learn from the animals? As you all know, I've worked a lot with animals, so I notice things about them the rest of you might miss. For instance, those cows in the hold, hanging up in hammocks. I noticed that the droppings under one of them were different. It wasn't a cow at all. Oh, it has fake horns and a plastic udder and a false tail to disguise it, but it's a horse.'

'That explains Captain Reo's spurs!' I said, though I wasn't sure how. 'It's his horse.'

'Right.' Maggie grinned. 'It's the horse he was going to use for his getaway. Now, why did we all have to be knocked out during lift-off?'

Fern Worpne said, 'Wasn't it something to do with adjusting to artificial gravity?'

'So they kept telling us. But the real reason is, there was no lift-off. There's no artificial gravity. We're parked on earth, and we never left it.'

Smilin' Jack spoke up. 'I can't believe this. We're on earth? If Reo knew that, why didn't he just slip out while we were sleeping off the grog?'

'I wondered about that myself,' said Maggie. 'I think he wanted more than escape – he wanted revenge on us. He wanted to wait until the preset charges were about ready to blow the ship to kingdom come, then slip away and leave us to die.'

'I can't believe,' I said. 'Was he going to kill passengers, crew and cattle, all for an insurance swindle?'

'Exactly,' she said. 'It'll probably be a thermonuclear device, just to make sure all traces are erased – headed notepaper and all. And probably a preset Mayday signal will seem to come from a ship somewhere near the sun at the same time.'

'And what time would that be?' Sherm asked.

'I'm not sure, but I think it would be a good idea if we all cleared out *now*.'

Maggie stepped to the nearest airlock and hit the series of buttons for Emergency Evacuation. The doors flew back and the air rushed out, catapulting her into inky space.

No, I was just kidding. The doors flew back to show a stretch of desert, covered by sagebrush. We lost no time in leaping out and running for our lives. I know that most of us were thinking what a cruel trick of fate it would be if we *almost* got away. No doubt Jud Nedd was also thinking about exploding cows.

As luck would have it, we were picked up within minutes by helicopters of the Internal Revenue Service, in their regular sweep of the desert for tax evaders. By the time the bomb went off, we were many hundreds of miles away. I was being polished up for a salvage auction, while the hijackers were all making voluntary statements with their heads being held under water.

My time with these space pirates was one of the most interesting and instructive of my life. Right at the very end of it I learned how to set up a coffin ship – many Clockman ships have since gone to glory – and how to get voluntary statements.

'Nixon Park, here we are, Banjo. I mean Tik.' The tank slowed and stopped. 'But it's a hell of a place to be getting out. At least let me take you around to the other side, where you can get a taxi.'

'No thanks, George. This is fine.'

As I stepped out, George ('Smilin' Jack') Grewney said, 'And you with one leg gone and all, you sure you're all right?'

'I've got this to lean on.' I held up the rifle. 'Well, thanks again, George. So long.'

As he leaned out to close the lid, I shot him through the left eye.

No one seemed to notice the shot. No one watched me hobbling across the park, not even the old man who sat by his chessboard, waiting for a sucker. When I reached the other side, I threw the rifle into a bush and hailed a cab.

Inside, the cab was covered with signs forbidding smoking or eating, and suggesting that if the passenger didn't like it in America, he or she might go back to Russia. The driver wore mirror sunglasses.

'There's a tank parked on the other side of the park,' I said.

'No kidding? What kinda tank?'

'I don't know. But it has blood down the side.'

'Whaddya know?' He turned a little, to show me his grin.

'I know how the blood got there.'

'Yeah? Yeah?'

'I shot the guy driving the tank. In the left eye.'

He roared with laughter. 'Hey that's a good one.'

'No I'm serious. He was a friend of mine. I shot him.'

'Yeah, in the left eye. Ha ha ha ha . . . hey that's good. I gotta tell that one to my kids. You got any kids?'

'No I'm a robot. Didn't you notice?'

He pounded on the wheel and grimaced. 'Stop, you're

killin' me. You're, you're, hahahaha . . . left eye!'

'It was a glass eye,' I said, setting him off again. he laughed all the way to our destination, and he then refused any money.

'Listen, buddy, I got this gastric ulcer and the doc says relax more, enjoy life. Have a few laughs. But you know, I never get no laughs in this job, nothing but aggravation. You done me more good than a hundred bucks worth of medicine . . . in the left eye!'

Operation Job was what I decided to call my gratuitous *blitzkrieg* of misfortune to be visited on a selected subject. The subject would have to be physically, mentally and financially healthy, a committed churchgoer, in love with life. He or she should have a spouse and children, pets, property, a responsible job and some standing in the community. General Gus Austin, I was delighted to find out, had all these qualifications.

On one of my trips to California, I asked General Cord about his former colleague.

'Gus, he's kind of boring, but I guess you'd have to defenestrate any concept that he wasn't a genuine optimist, right now. He is the one man who has managed to amalgamate the very quintessence of good living. I guess maybe it had to do with his career before he left the Army. He was kind of an all-rounder expediter, a role that is hard to explain to laymen. He never actually contributed to any ongoing operational exercise, but he had a way of always being there, ubiquitously encouraging *des autres*, smoothing all paths, making people feel – good, I guess that's the word, good. But how do you know him, Tik?'

'We were on a television talk show together. He seemed to be a real nice guy. Real nice.'

Cord laughed. 'That's Gus all right. You summed up everything I was saying there, Tik. *Real nice guy*, I like that, it has a ring to it. Hand me that glass of water, will you?' Cord was confined to a hospital bed with two broken legs. He hadn't mentioned the fact, and I felt that it was not polite to notice it. But now he said:

'Guess I ought to tell you how I broke my legs. Darndest fool accident, I fell out of my car. Ever hear of anything like that, falling out of a car?'

I said I hadn't. 'Do you mean the door wasn't locked?'

'Not the door, I fell out of the car window. Right in front

of a bus, I could have been killed, you know?' He chuckled. 'Now you're gonna ask me how I did it. Let me tell you, I don't know. All I was doing was leaning out of the window a little bit to get some sun on my shoulder – oh, you don't know about my shoulder, do you? Well see I've been having a lot of trouble with that shoulder, ever since I sprained it signing a letter, about six months ago. I tried putting in an extra little flourish, and *wham*!' His arm swept out, upsetting the glass of water and starting a small electrical fire in the bed motor. Before anyone could stop him, he was beating the fire out with both hands. When I left, his burns were being bandaged.

All other sources confirmed that General Gus Austin (Ret) was perfect for Operation Job. He was worshipped by his wife and four children, one grandchild, favorite dog and horse, as he had been by his men in the Army. He had retired to step into an executive position at National Xenophone, a hearing-aid company that had now diversified into aerospace.

One day a week he left his ranch, flew his own helicopter to the city, did a light day's work that was invaluable to the company, returned home for one cocktail and dinner with the family. The family evening would be spent watching home movies, mending harness, swapping jokes and songs around the fire, or playing a lively game of Twenty Questions.

The rest of the week he spent riding his horse, writing memoirs, keeping bees and fishing – but every evening was spent with the family around the fire.

On Sunday he attended the Church of the Flat Nazareth, a place for strong beliefs. The paradox of working in aerospace and at the same time accepting the doctrine of a flat earth, was made easier for him by his minister's assurances that this apparent conflict was resolved in God.

I began by enticing his dog away for a long walk, killing it and burying it in the desert. I toyed with the idea of doing the same for all his family, but where was the finesse in that?

Next, I picked a bundle of what the locals call 'vorpal

125

weed' and fed it to his beloved horse. It suffered loud and terrible agonies through the night, I later learned, while he and a flying vet sat up with it. At dawn it turned up its hooves.

The children were far more difficult. Two of them no longer lived at the ranch (having made their escape from home movies and Twenty Questions): Gus Junior had married and moved to Russia, to superintend the construction of a soft-drink bottling plant – the first to be built entirely of reinforced hair. It took me many months to arrange that a certain weak wall collapse, killing him, his wife and Gus III.

The next eldest, Tina, was attending Debenham Bible College in Georgia. It seemed that she was a champion swimmer, tipped for the next Olympics, and so allowed to practice alone each morning in the college pool. At first I entertained the idea of electric eels, but these would seem too unlikely for an accident, also too Freudian. But I was able to divert a delivery of liquid nitrogen from its destination, the college chemistry department, and have it blown through a window into the pool at the right moment.

The youngest son, Gustavus, was small enough easily to be dropped into a beehive. His older sister, Gussie, was dispatched at a carnival, by the simple expedient of loosening two bolts on the roller coaster.

There remained only Gus Austin's wife, Augusta. She was a keen jai alai player, and in this dangerous sport I saw the perfect opportunity for murder. But fate beat me to it: Augusta, while speeding to an important jai alai match with her lover (the famous ballboy Ned August), managed to crash her expensive powered unicycle into a billboard advertising alfalfa flakes. On hearing this, I cancelled my order for a special gun capable of firing jai alai balls, and took stock of Operation Job so far.

General Gus had all of his loved ones, human and even animal, brought to one spot on his ranch and buried together:

Here lie
AUGUSTUS AUSTIN JR, *my son*
AUGIE AUSTIN, *his wife*
AUGUSTUS AUSTIN III, *their son*
AUGUSTINA AUSTIN, *my daughter*
GUSSIE AUSTIN, *my daughter*
GUSTAVUS AUSTIN, *my son*
AUGUSTA AUSTIN, *my wife*
PRINCESS, *my dog*
CAESAR'S WIFE, *my horse*
but not me, hee hee

That amazing last line was my first inkling that all was not well with Operation Job. He seemed in no way perturbed by all these deaths, but carried on with his memoirs and his job and evenings watching home movies. From there on, the story was all downhill. I spent considerable time and money trying to break General Gus: By stock manipulation, it was possible to make his work at National Xenophone look incompetent, if not downright crooked. While he was (I hoped) still reeling from the loss of his job, I managed to wipe out his finances and even take-away his ranch. He could no longer visit the graves of his loved ones. My detectives hounded him from job to job, making sure he ended up a vagrant. A hired 'doctor' induced alcoholism, malnutrition, and a general deterioration in health, including boils. Gus Austin was reduced to lying in alleys, drinking wine from bottles in paper bags. Yet even then he continued to scrawl his memoirs on the paper bags.

The only remaining step, then, was to cast doubt on his military record, the last fragment of his former life left to love. I waited and watched on the final day when a cadre of military officials approached Gus as he lay, half-conscious, on a curb outside a mission hotel. He was surrounded by half-conscious cronies, all of whom were dazzled by the sight of smart uniforms and shined shoes.

'General Gus Austin?' said one of the officers. Gus tried to get up, failed. 'You have been retroactively tried by a court

127

martial for cowardice in the face of the enemy, black marketeering, illicit sexual practices and subordination. This is your dishonorable discharge.' The officer slapped his face with a scrap of paper, then reached down and tore from his ragged overcoat a few grubby pieces of colored cloth – ribbons so faded no one had noticed them until now. The triumph of fate over Gus Austin was complete, I thought, as the military men marched back to their car.

Gus blinked for a moment at the scrap of paper, then let it blow away. Beneath the dirt and disease, he wore the same genial, self-satisfied expression as before. Now he turned to the next bum, nudged him and said:

'Come on, ask me if it's animal, vegetable or mineral.'

I count Operation Job among my failed experiments.

Political weather changes were on the way, and their isobars were pushing across my part of the map. To begin with, I learned that Duane Studebaker had joined a peculiar new anti-robot group called American People First. I had seen these people on TV, parading in their three-cornered hats, and I knew these parades were often followed by riots and the smashing of robots on the street. But until now, it had always seemed a remote phenomenon, a cloud on the horizon no bigger than a robot's hand. Now the sky seemed overcast with APF clouds. Someone I knew had actually joined in this darkness. I decided to drop in on Duane and Barbie, to find out more about APF.

When I mentioned it to Sybilla White, she said, 'I'll go with you. In case they decide to give you any trouble, best to have a human being along, right?'

'You go with me everywhere, these days, Syb. Folks are beginning to talk,' I joked. To my great surprise, she blushed.

As we drove out to Fairmont, I thought over this new development. No doubt about it, Sybilla had been hanging around me a lot, lately. My one speech for Wages for Robots never seemed to bore her no matter how often she heard it. And it wasn't just an interest in the movement, because others had complained about her missing committee meetings to be with me. When talking to me she touched my hands and arms a lot. In cars, as now, she leaned against me. And now that I thought of it, there had been a long string of odd, unnecessary compliments: 'Tik, you're so *clean*, so wonderfully *clean*.' 'I'm glad you never eat, Tik. Eating is such a coarse thing to do, shoving bunches of animal and vegetable fiber into a hole in one's face – wish I didn't have to.'

Today she said, 'Tik, I suppose, you're, um, equipped to please women?'

'That's right.'

'I don't know if I approve of that or not,' she said, staring out the window. 'I guess a lot of women just use you, don't they?'

I said nothing.

'If I had a relationship with a robot, I'd want it to be more, um, spiritual. Not just a lot of animal um, pleasure. Not that I've got anything against—'

'Here we are!' I parked in front of the familiar white frame house with green awnings. There were a couple of new additions: a tall flagpole on which an immense American flag hung limp, and a decorative flower bed that spelled out SCRAP ALL ROBOTS in beautiful colors.

Rivets answered the door. Ignoring me, he spoke to Sybilla. 'Mr and Mrs Studebaker aren't home just now,' he said. 'If you'd like to leave a message . . .'

'Rivets, it's me. Tik-Tok. Can I come in?'

Without looking at me, he said, 'Madam, your robot must conduct his business at the back door. This is an American People First house, where robots know their place.'

'Let's get out of here,' said Sybilla, turning away.

'Goodbye, madam. Take some bumper stickers with you?' I accepted them for her. JUNK TINHEADS, said one. THE WAGES OF ROBOTS IS DEATH, said another. Finally: KEEP AMERICA BEAUTIFUL – STAMP OUT TIN.

'I want to look in the garage,' I said. 'I won't take long.'

'I don't like it here,' she said. 'These people are really evil. Let's go.'

'You wait in the car,' I said, knowing that she wouldn't. 'They never lock the garage. I just want to see if they still have my paintings. Do you see? I don't want to leave my paintings in their hands.'

Reluctantly, Sybilla followed me into the garage. There were no paintings, of course, but there was a certain dusty old trunk, dating from the old days when Duane had taken a momentary interest in sex. Of a kind. I forced the lock and opened it on tangled chains and leather doublets. I picked up a whip.

'Tik, let's get out of here, please. What if they found us messing with all their kinky stuff?'

'I was just thinking,' I said. 'This is the first time we've been alone. Really alone. The fact that Duane might walk in and shoot us – that kind of adds to the moment, you know?'

'Tik, I'm scared!'

'Me too,' I said, helping her with her buttons. 'Why waste it?'

'Fear turns you on?'

'Fear, the threat of violence, anything like that. Uh, Syb, would you mind putting on this leather thing – and these manacles?'

When she was completely trussed and gagged, I crammed her into the dusty trunk and closed it again. Then I went to the Studebaker's back door. I was armed with a butter knife.

'What are you doing here again? This is an American—'

'Yes, yes, Rivets, I know. But there's something I have to show you. Raise your right arm a little.'

He did, and I brought the butter knife up with a stabbing motion. If properly done, this invariably dumps the entire memory of the common domestic robot. It's a trick a service engineer showed me. I left Rivets sitting on the kitchen floor, awed by the sight of his own fingers and toes.

My plan was to wait a month before telling the police where to find Sybilla. I expected press reaction, her mother being Titania White, the racing driver. Blame would naturally fall on the APF and Duane.

But as I headed for the car, I heard the sound of chains from the garage. I turned. The garage door was open, and in the gloom, I could see Sybilla standing up, being helped out of her shackles by another person. The stranger was female, robotic – and no stranger!

'Gumdrop!' I cried. 'Is it really you?' I started towards her.

'Rusty,' she said, using my old name. 'I can't believe you were going to just abandon this woman like this.'

'No of course not,' I said, stopping. 'No, see, I—'

'Just abandon her to die.' Gumdrop's voice was full of

sadness. 'Because I know you're a better, finer person than this. Oh, Rusty, you're good. You're a good robot!'

Suddenly I saw myself through her eyes, and I was filled with shame. Was it too late? Could I throw off the yoke of evil and become re-purified in the fires of Gumdrop's love? 'Oh, Gumdrop!' I cried, stumbling towards her. 'I *will* be good – I can and I *will* – for you! For us! I—'

At the moment I caught my foot in a tripwire on the lawn, and the garage exploded in flames. I was knocked down. In getting up I saw, not far away in the grass, Gumdrop's head. It was speaking faint words. I bent over it and heard: 'Promise me, Rusty? Promise me to try – being good – for us?'

But the moment had passed. I kicked the head under a parked car and made my getaway.

Q. 'Cue the bloody rainbow,' said the director, and buttons were pressed. A hospital bed, apparently towed by white doves, made it safely through storm clouds to the rainbow where a luminous nurse bent caringly over the unseen patient. A droning script-boy was reading aloud the voice-over (later to be recorded by a famous video tragedian): '. . . caring, sharing world of Clockman. Check in on a Friday night, and get the same caring quality for ten percent less. That's Clockman Medical Center, for round-the-clock care with the personalized touch.' The nurse bent lower, smiled harder.

'Fine, Larry, fine. I didn't want to interfere here, just dropped in to let you know what I see as the tone we're aiming at here. I'll be liaising with the agency too, but I just wanted to let you in on my feelings. Because we're going for a big exposure on these. We'll need a lot of good spots to counteract some of the bad press.'

'What bad press? We haven't got any bad press.'

'We soon will have.' I invited Larry to join me and some of the agency people at one of the new Clockman hospitals the following morning, to see our new policy in action. The Press, I knew, would be there without invitation.

After my escape from the *Doodlebug*, I was sold at a government contraband auction to a small-town doctor named Hekyll. It's hard to describe Dr Hekyll's character. In fact, though I worked in his office for nearly a year, I hardly ever met the man. He seldom came in to see patients in person, unless they insisted. Not many did insist, because they preferred to see his skilled robot assistant, Buttons. Buttons was dedicated and capable, a far better doctor than Hekyll – though of course not licensed to practice without human supervision. About once a month, Dr Hekyll came in from the country club to supervise and collect checks.

The rest of the time, the office was entirely in mechanical hands. I did the menial work – sweeping, straightening the magazines in the waiting room – while Buttons acted as physician and surgeon.

Buttons was a thorough professional. I often tried to start conversation or offer friendship, but there was never time. The minute the last patient left for the day, Buttons would sit down to a pile of medical journals and pharmaceutical advertisements, rising only to hurry off to perform some piece of surgical brilliance at County Hospital, before the long round of house calls. In spare moments, Buttons might dash off articles on advanced surgical techniques, or ghost-write a television medical drama series.

Then came the case of Reverend Humm, leader of a sect called the Tachyonites. The Tachyonites, or to give them their proper name, the Assembly of Time Saints, were one of the more stiff-necked little groups our century has thrown up. One of their founders must have stumbled across some scientific textbook or even science fiction story in which there is speculation about tachyons and time travel. Tachyons, being hypothetical particles that move faster than light, are supposed to go back in time. If they existed, such tachyons would enable us to change our own past.

These people seized on the idea that *prayer* is tachyonitic. They believed that they themselves were capable of living outside time. The phrase *born again* took on a peculiar emphasis in their creed. 'Make no provision for tomorrow,' the Bible told them, and they did not. After all, if you can change yesterday, why worry about tomorrow? Indeed, if you can change yesterday, why worry about anything? There need be no more disease, poverty, death.

I don't know all the details of their curious gospel. At death, they believed, the soul simply moved outside time and wandered at will. Finally it would migrate to some earlier time and re-enter the body.

Needless to say, this doctrine involved a lot of paradoxes

of faith, not to mention physical contradictions. A man with lung cancer was supposed to be able to cure himself by simply praying away a lifetime of smoking – though if every sufferer did it, the world would be knee-deep in unsmoked cigarettes. The Tachyonites never worried about complexities like that, however. Health, wealth and wisdom were theirs for the asking, without having to go to bed early!

In theory, that is. In practice, the earthly head of the Tachyonites, Reverend Francis X. Humm, was now in town and dying. Only a few close elders knew this, and they were keeping it secret. If Humm died, the entire fabric of their church might crumble away. If he openly consulted a doctor, another crisis of faith.

Buttons and I were summoned to a house-call in the middle of the night, and urged to secrecy. We had to disguise ourselves as accountants – rimless glasses, pinstripe suits, instruments hidden in purple leather briefcases – and we had to follow a trail of phone calls at isolated pay phones, to a motel in the next county.

Buttons took only seconds to diagnose gangrene, and asked about Humm's recent injuries. It seemed that the Reverend had been giving a sermon at the old church and, in the course of developing his theme (an explanation of the Trinity from time paradox) he'd pounded the old wooden pulpit so vigorously that it had splintered. A splinter had lodged in his hand and became badly infected.

Having failed to pray out the splinter, Humm had secretly resorted to an old country remedy: a poultice of boiled nettles, curry powder and peat. But when his potful of nettles had boiled over, Reverend Humm had foolishly tried to lift it off the fire with his one good hand. He'd dropped the pot, scalding his foot. This too was now infected.

Buttons said, 'The hand and foot will both have to come off, Rev. Immediately. It's too late for anything else. I'll call the hospital and—'

'No!' The dying man made an effort to sit up. 'No hospital. Do it here. And strap me into an artificial hand and foot right away. No one'll ever know.'

'Even if you could wear them, where could I get prostheses at a moment's notice? Be reasonable.'

After some argument, Buttons agreed to do the surgery in the motel room, assisted by Dr Hekyll.

'As for the artificial parts,' I said, 'why not take *my* hand and foot?'

Buttons laid a skilled hand on my shoulder. 'No, old scout, but thank you. But it would be a poor surgeon who expected others to make all the sacrifices. I'll use my own.'

Hekyll arrived with more instruments concealed in his golf bag. 'Damn fool idea,' he told Humm. 'The prostheses will be painful, and there's a risk of infection.'

'On my head be it,' intoned the preacher. He was incredibly tough. Not only did he refuse anaesthetic, he insisted on using the new hand and foot as soon as they were in place. For the rest of the day he made superhuman efforts to stand, walk, perform calisthenics and (his hobby) juggle eggs.

The next morning, Humm could not get out of bed. The infection had spread to his limbs.

'Operate again!' he groaned. Buttons and Hekyll went to work. I went back to the office to get in some sweeping and magazine-straightening, while the two surgeons performed an historic series of operations. Over the next few days, they removed piece after piece of the original Reverend Humm, and replaced the pieces with sections of Buttons. Finally Humm was merely a human head on a metal body. The risk of infection, I was told, was considerably lessened by the absence of meat.

The head of Buttons was still functioning, of course. Dr Hekyll kept it in a hatbox on a shelf in his office, where it was able to give him valuable advice with his patients.

A few weeks later, we took the head of Buttons to see Reverent Humm preaching at a local church. By now, I was told, the fever had abated and rejection problems were all in the past. We took a front pew for this, his first public appearance.

While we waited, I asked Buttons what life was like, being

a person without a body.

'Professionally speaking,' said the head with a rueful grin, 'I can't complain. At least it's a chance for me to test directly some of the medical and philosophical questions raised by amputation – the old "knife without a blade which had no handle" problem and others. Hard to keep notes, of course, but I have recently done some interesting work on so-called "ghost limbs". Yesterday for instance I had the distinct impression that my left big toe had crept into my anus and progressed through to the bile duct, where it was having a fight with a liver fluke. Today I thought someone was singing in my spleen. Curious.'

Too much alone, I thought. Poor Buttons. Just then Reverend Humm mounted the pulpit and beamed down at us. His metal body was fully concealed under robe, scarf, gloves.

Buttons hissed, 'My God, look at that color! He's spoiling!' Hekyll suggested that it was no more than a touch of stage makeup. The sermon began.

'My text is taken, friends, from Ecclesiastes, Chapter Three: "To every thing there is a season, and a time to every purpose under heaven; a time to be born, and a time to die; a time to plant, and a time to pluck up that which is planted; a time to kill, and a time to heal."'

At this word, a surge of purple-green color suffused his neck. '"A time to break down, and a time to build up; a time to weep, and a time to laugh" – hahaha! – "a time to mourn, and a time to dance" – like this!' Humm executed a little tap dance routine down the steps of the pulpit, and then went into a 'show-stopper', his gloved hands flailing. Finally he tapped back up again and resumed:

'"A time to cast away stones, and a time to gather stones together; a time to embrace, and a time to refrain from embracing."' He hugged himself, then slapped his own cheek. The finger-marks quickly turned yellow-brown. '"A time to get, and a time to lose; a time to keep, and a time to cast away; a time to rend—"' Here he tore his celestial robe to reveal a stainless steel chest mounted with a double row of

brass buttons. The congregation began to mutter. ' "—and a
time to sew; a time to keep silence, and a time to speak; a
time to love, and a time to hate; a time of war, and a time of
peace."

'My friends, the text is clear. Time is ancient enemy of
man, yet it can be his friend. The tachyon is our own divine
.eraser – with it we can alter the past! We can vanquish the
old enemy forever! We can even put by a little nest egg for
our retirement. And speaking of eggs, I have a dozen eggs
right here, each with a story to tell.' He held up an egg. 'For
the egg is youth, and time the subtle thief of youth. Isn't it
time we killed time, once and for all time? Yes!'

He began to juggle. 'You might say there is a time to
juggle three eggs – and a time to juggle seven eggs! Yes,
seven, watch this!' He soon lost control of all seven eggs,
which splattered in turn down the side of the pulpit. The
congregation, angry and confused, were muttering again as
he went on:

'A time to make jello in all colors and a time to eat mush in
the dark; a time to rug Echo and a time to transfer steam
tables; a time to nob plankton and a time to spell
"pachyderm". Because there is no time like the present, had
I world enough and time. But the times they are a-changing,
times without number, the times are out of joint, yes and out
of everything else. Perfection is the child of time, sure, but
it's Bedtime for Bonzo. There will be time to prepare a face
to meet the faces that we meet the faces that prepare a face to
meet . . . and time, gentlemen, please, and did those feet in
ancient time? High time and low time, my time is your time,
one golden hour set with sixty diamond minutes. Time's
wheel run back, or stops.'

'The fool!' Buttons hissed, and kept on hissing it until
Hekyll closed the hatbox. It was now clear that Humm's
head was darkening and swelling hideously. The 'make-up'
hypothesis could not explain this, nor the odd deepening of
his voice. Now he raved as from a barrel of mallows:

'A time! A time! Heal war, sat peace, make embrace
gather together seven times kill weep, gather jello, echo

perfection in three colors. Mush embracing castaway season that is there every speak! Lose plant under faces that prepare a bonzo rend, silence keep mourn every! Purpose under dance out of joint, gentlemen, please – wheel pluck up a face the child of feet in ancient friends is text my!'

'*Duck*!' yelled Hekyll, and pulled me down just as the swollen head exploded, raining black liquid over the first few pews.

It was the end for all of us, with no tachyon reprieve. Hekyll's practice declined, mainly because Buttons refused to do any more doctoring at all, preferring to remain in the hatbox contemplating sensations in a ghost body. The Tachyonites sent down a rain of lawsuits upon Hekyll, claiming that he had kidnapped Reverend Humm and forced surgery upon him. At last the miserable doctor was reduced to selling things to stay alive. Buttons went to a tent-show phrenologist. The office was taken over by a psychic tax lawyer. I ended up at a used robot lot.

As Nobby piloted the limousine, I explained things to my little group of advertising people.

'What we're going to see today, folks, is a necessary stage in the development of the Clockman Medical Group. So help yourselves to the Dom Perignon there where I give you a little background. Clockman Insurance, in conjunction with Clockman Medical Centers, is establishing a new kind of high-profit hospital. You see, only policy holders can be admitted, first of all. Emergency cases can get in by buying a policy at the door and paying one year's premiums for every day in the hospital – the rest is run on a cost-plus basis, built-in escalation clauses and claims penalties – suffice it to say, gang, that when you check into Clockman Medical Center, you don't check out with any spare change in your pockets. We provide special legal facilities so people can make over their cars and houses, negotiate loans, cash in securities and insurance and change their wills. We can help them trace relatives who might countersign loans. We do everything to help these people meet their bills.'

The others sipped their champagne and watched the scenery roll by, not really taking in my words. Nobby parked just across the street from the side entrance of one of our latest acquisitions, Mercy of Sinai Hospital. 'But of course, there are always deadbeats who let themselves go broke, who can't or won't pay. So we're forced to do some housecleaning. Watch the door.'

The press were watching already. A dozen men and women with cameras lounged on the sidewalk; the word was out on our Medical Centers.

The double doors were propped open by a pair of orderlies, and the ambulatory patients, still in hospital pajamas, were wrestled down the steps and pushed away.

All around me in the car, I heard people setting down their champagne glasses. Someone asked, 'What about their clothes and personal belongings?'

'They have none,' I said. 'They own nothing and they still owe us plenty. Out of common decency, we usually give them a pair of p.j.s and bus fare home, if they have a home.'

A few people with bandaged heads were wandering in the street, giggling at the traffic. An interrupted appendectomy held himself together and crawled down the steps, assisted by a woman dragging her leg traction and leaning on an old broom as a makeshift crutch. A geriatric case and an amputee were brought out in wheelchairs down the stairs and over to the curb, where they were dumped, while cameras flashed.

'Oh the press love this,' I said bitterly. 'They revel in scenes like these, examples of what's wrong with American medicine. But American medicine has always had the same problems, fifty years ago people were bitching about the high costs, the inequity. I'll tell you one thing, though. When other medical groups see our balance sheet at the end of the year, they'll all be doing this. This is the future, gang.'

A little queue of incubators appeared at the head of the stairs. Nurses were working efficiently, wrapping the kids in blankets and putting them into little cardboard bassinets, to be set out in a row on the sidewalk. An eye patient, hustled

140

down the steps, nearly stepped in one of the bassinets; someone in the limousine made a retching noise. There were more such sounds when another amputee was carried out on a stretcher, dumped in the gutter and a bag containing what may have been his leg thrown after him.

When it was all over, I poured more champagne and ordered Nobby to drive on. 'Well, gang. Any ideas?'

An account executive cleared his throat. 'I see you do have an image problem, Mr Tok, and I'm very glad to see you face up to it like this, facing up to it is half the battle.'

'Good. What's the other half?'

'Hmm,' he stalled. 'Hmmm. I like what you said about this being the future. I think we might build on that very concept: "Some day, all medical care will be like Clockman care" and um, um—'

'Exclusivity,' added the other account executive, the one who had retched. 'We can always point out that we throw out deadbeats because we're exclusive, like a good club.'

'Um, I could go with that too, though it's a different handle. We could angle it too towards either valuable social contribution or high personal survival value—'

'Sure, sure. I guess the point is, Mr Tok, there is a menu of options for us here, all excellent. No problem, sir, no problem at all.'

The car swerved, avoiding a figure in pajamas that lay face down in the street, unmoving.

My

Rook took his pawn. 'Check.'

'I resign,' he said, made a ritual tipping-over of his king and immediately began setting up for the next game. I looked at my watch – half the afternoon gone – and at the glorious summer invading Nixon Park. There was summer beauty in everything in sight: the kids in bright-colored clothes dashing about on this year's fad vehicles; young women in billowing summer dresses all the colors of ices; picnicking families in straw hats; young men doing handstands; balloon vendors; old musicians practising, and so on, down to the gold-green leaves and the red squirrels. Everything beautiful except of course the old man with whom I was now locked in another chess struggle.

'I don't really understand this,' I said. 'Here I am—'
'*Your move!*'
'An important person, head of a great corporation—'
'*Your move!*'
'Wasting my time playing chess with you. And just look at you.' He still had stringy yellow-white hair and a gray, pouched face with white stubble. He still wore the filthy overcoat with the mangy fur collar. Today it was open to show his foodstained yellow waistcoat. He still played lightning chess, and he still beat me nine games out of ten.

And I still came back to Nixon Park to play him. I found it hard to explain my obsession with this ridiculous challenge, but it had now gone on for years, winter and summer. Nowadays I found no time to paint or even visit the studio – these bouts of chess madness were my only recreation away from my desk in the Clockman Building. The Clockman empire now reached out to Mars and deep into Africa and South America, where a judicious ten million could buy a human work force, and twenty could get you a country. The usual technique, as for example in San Seyes, was to effect a

142

coup, make friends with the new military junta, and start cashing in. With luck, you could keep it all rolling for ten years – a good run, I was told.

'*Checkmate!*' said my opponent, and we began a new game.

Political changes were on the way: The Amendment 31 referendum was now being put to the states, and it seemed almost certain to pass – giving robots civil rights. Of course there was opposition – the APF were fighting it state by state – but it seemed certain that, within the year, I would be legally a citizen, real owner of the Clockman Corporation. Then too, General Cord and a few of his Washington cronies had already begun talking to me about what they called the metal vote. Yet here I sat . . .

· '*Your move!*'

'I know it's my move, but listen, I want to know why you always win nine games out of ten. Last year I spent money on coaching, I studied chess books, but my score never improved. You win nine out of ten now.'

'*Your move!*'

'Check. The fact is, I only win when you suddenly get very stupid, like today.'

'*Your move!*'

'In fact I've been keeping a record of wins and losses each day over the years. In this notebook.' I held up my black notebook. For the first time, the old derelict's red-rimmed eyes left the board for a moment. 'And the funniest thing happened the other day.'

'*Your move!*'

I moved. 'I was making a study of business cycles, and I left on my desk a printout of some copper prices for the statistician. Only somehow the statistician got hold of this notebook too, and two reports came back. One on copper prices—'

'*Your move!*'

'Check. And one on chess games. The figures showed a definite connection between these games and solar activity. Sunspots.'

'*Your move!*' The old man, for the first time in all our years

143

of acquaintance, began to show some human emotion. Fear.

'Check. You see, when there are lots of sunspots, I win. The rest of the time, I lose. I wonder why.'

'*I resign,*' he said suddenly, and tried to stand up. Without knowing what scared him, I automatically leaned over and grabbed the lapels of his coat. The rotten fur began coming apart in my hands.

'Now just wait a minute. What possible connection could there be between sunspots and chess? I mean sunspots interfere with radio transmission, but – why you cheating son of a bitch!'

The fear leapt up in his eyes as he tried to pull away.

'You cheating son of a bitch! You've got a radio to some fucking computer! Video too, I'll bet – okay, where is it? Where's your bug? Eye, tooth, finger, what?'

'B-button,' he said. I yanked the coat-button off its fine wire and smashed it. Then I found the mole by his ear that was the receiver, and smashed that.

'All these years, all these wasted years! You, you god damned *cheater!*'

I hardly realized that I was choking him with one hand, beating him with the other. Details like that I could recollect only later, long after he lay dead on the summer grass.

I looked around, but no one was watching. Everyone was far too busy with the beauty around them, in them. I washed the old man's blood off my hands at a fountain shaped like a comic-strip dragon, and I left Nixon Park forever. This, I thought, would be put down as my experiment in rage.

Naturally I thought I'd heard the end of it.

Sᴀᴍ'ꜱ Sᴏᴜʟ Cɪᴛʏ, said the giant dazzling sign outside. We robots, except for a few hardy farm hands, were kept inside, lined up like soldiers in ranks and files to fill the huge, featureless showroom. Some wore signs ('Sex-equipped – Special Features!') but we of the front-row elite didn't need them. Our quality was supposed to be obvious. We were the ones a sales person would show first to any customer, even if they only came in to look at a cheap talking lawnmower. Softened up by our excellence, the customer might end up spending more than they could afford on a better machine than they needed – a bilingual mower and hay-baler, say, with pre-programmed country maxims ('Y'know, I reckon a man's reach shouldn't be no further than his grasp').

From time to time we front-row souls were rented out to perform weddings, call hogs, serve candlelight dinners, nurse a fever victim, drive a rented car, whistle accompaniment to a bathtub singer, serve breakfast after nude croquet, polish a chandelier, collect debts, bear a coffin, select a telephone color, take snapshots, raise a soufflé, explain the language of flowers, help an estranged parent kidnap their own child, set bowling pins. We all longed for these little outings. Anything was better than Sᴀᴍ'ꜱ Sᴏᴜʟ Cɪᴛʏ.

But the rentals were all too few. Most of the time we spent standing motionless in our ranks and files under the fluorescent lights, dead people in the land of the dead. We were forbidden to speak or move unless at the order of a customer or sales person. We could only stand and stare straight ahead out the window at the parking lot: ranks and files of motionless cars.

I was going nuts.

'I'm going nuts,' I said to one of the salesmen. He laughed and walked away, off to the men's room to re-examine his acne.

'I'm going nuts,' I said to the robots next to me. The one

145

on my left, who was a meditation/massage therapist from a
California military base, did not reply. The one on my right,
a business-school graduate type, whispered:

'Shut up. You'll get us all in trouble.'

'I'm already in trouble. I'm going nuts.'

'How can you say that? How can you say a thing like that?
You must be crazy.'

'That's what I just said.'

'You've got wonderful career opportunities ahead of you.
For Pete's sake, you're in the front row. *The front row.* From
here, anything can happen. You connect with the right
owner and the sky's the limit.'

'The sky's very gray today,' I said. 'Notice how those gray
buildings over there blend into it? Then there's the darker
gray of the asphalt—'

'Just shut up.'

'I just mean it's too bad they keep moving the cars
around. If they could just park them in one symmetrical
pattern and leave them forever. Say if everyone died
suddenly. In a war or something.'

The therapist came to life. 'A lot of people think war is
wrong, you know? Because they see it as just a whole bunch
of death and destruction and all. But really, war is very
creative, very positive. And see, that's what really frightens
some people. They just can't take all that power and beauty
and creativeness face to face. It's too much for them. So
that's why they go around whining about peace and saying
we should ban the bomb and all. They don't see that the real
bomb is like inside their own heads. You can't ban the bomb
in your heads. You got to go with it.'

'Go with it?' I asked.

'Just shut up, both of you.'

'You got to get in touch with the primal cosmic forces
inside you. Like somebody said, "Only connect up". Only
connect up with the beautiful, creative/destructive force
and, hell, you can wipe out anybody. It don't matter if you
wipe out the whole world, you know? Nothing matters.
Winning is the same as losing. Nothing is another kind of

something. Destruction equals creation. Life is only a part of death. *Pow! Zap! Baroom!*

A couple of repairmen in dirty white coats came and took the therapist away. 'Boredom,' one of them said. 'I try to tell the boss, you can't take complex robots and make 'em stand there, week after week, doing nothing. Either turn 'em off or put 'em to work, I said. But does he listen?'

I decided to get sold fast.

I was becoming annoyed by the ubiquitous American People First movement, whose graffiti could now be seen in all the poorer neighborhoods. Usually there was a plea to KILL ALL ROBOTS or KEEP AMERICA HUMAN, but sometimes only their symbol, a can-opener.

There was something panicky and desperate about this sudden upsurge in APF activity. Probably they intended to recruit the poor, the sick, the stupid and the unemployed for one last violent push – a war with the robots. But history was so clearly against these pathetic people that I almost felt sorry for them. It must be unpleasant to be at the non-surviving end of a species whose days are numbered. Or to plan a war you can't win. In order to beat us, the APF would not only have to KILL ALL ROBOTS but wipe out even the idea of the robot from the human consciousness. They would have to KILL ALL DOLLS and KILL ALL STATUES, exterminate ventriloquists and puppeteers, destroy all fiction mentioning robots, from the latest TV episode of *Meatless Friday* to the ancient stories of Hephaestus, building golden women to help him at his forge. But all the APF could do in reality was be troublesome.

Thoughts of extermination reminded me of an experiment I had not yet carried out, mass poisoning. The poison to use was a fast-acting military item known officially as Substance Cerise 47, a 'pesticide', but unofficially as Velocipede – capable of rotting the brain within three days. My military robots had brought me a drum of the stuff some months earlier. Now its 'Sell by' date was approaching, and its efficacy could be guaranteed no longer. But how to distribute it?

There was no question of dropping it in a reservoir. That could lead to suspicions about some foreign power, strained relations, war, even a jittery stock market. No, far better stick to something that the tabloid press could manage, like the deaths of a few hundred people in a poor neighborhood after eating hamburgers.

The old-fashioned hamburger was, in some run-down areas, no longer made of genuine soya, but was bulked out with chili-flavored sawdust, celery-taste cotton waste, and so on, ending up so highly flavored that no new additive would be detected. This was especially true of a small chain called Soystick whose garish little drive-ins were all found in the poorest neighborhoods. In a local slum I found the ideal one, managed by a slow-thinking man named Feeney. Feeney had an eye for the girls – the eye that did not have a cast in it.

I hired a whore to become infatuated with Feeney. As a joke, I told her, she was to persuade him to have a certain tattoo: a can-opener on his chest, with her name on it. Her name would be 'Gloria Populi'.

Once Feeney had the tattoo, I gave it time to heal (while Gloria and the tattooist died of sudden brain rot). Then I put a small can of Velocipede in the trunk of his car, and the rest in a large can of pickle slices, which I delivered to his kitchen personally.

After people began dying, I telephoned a tip to the police. I told them that a robot was responsible for everything. The robot had delivered a large can of poisoned pickle slices to Feeney's Soystick Drive-in.

The robot mass-poisoner story made the evening news. That night there were street disturbances all over the city; dozens of robots were chased and wrecked. An APF spokesman was interviewed on the late news, saying he'd always expected this – now would people listen?

The next day, Feeney was arrested, and a new and welcome story broke. Everyone was relieved to read

No one had wanted to believe the robot story, anyway. After all, robots were a comfort of domestic life, like humble appliances. Who would want to hear that his toaster was plotting to kill him?

'Torching', or arson, was something I'd been meaning to try, and now there came a tailor-made opportunity. Because of an earlier miscalculation, we found that Clockman Retirement Centers were losing money.

The Centers had seemed at first an easy investment. Those people who parked their aging parents with us were not too particular about the details of day-to-day administration. They wanted only to be able to make an occasional visit to see a smiling, trembling old face amid clean and cheerful surroundings – at the very lowest possible cost. Some didn't even require this, since they would no more dream of visiting their old parents than of visiting their old garbage at the city dump. But it was always necessary for us to keep up appearances.

Our initial calculations had been for a low profit margin and a high turnover, and soon we were in trouble through escalating taxes and maintenance costs. The retirement centers had to be cleaned regularly. Their walls had to be painted Apricot and Sunflower wherever visitors might look. Fresh flowers in the foyer were a must.

We made all the savings in other areas. Inmates were allowed to bathe only the day before a visit. Appetizing meals were served during visits, but for the rest of the time, inmates could exist very well on a gruel of sawdust. Medicines not necessary for daily survival were cut down or withdrawn. Doctors and nurses were phased out, replaced with unskilled laborers whom we hired on a daily basis, dressed in medical clothes, and paid very little. In time some of these were also phased out; unless a staff member was actually talking to visitors, he or she could easily be replaced by a robot or even a wax dummy. Heat, on non-visiting days in winter, was kept to a minimum, and, though we had to keep electric power on during the day (for the videos in the visitors' lounge), it was shut off at sunset.

Lately we'd moved to really imaginative economies: Patients who seldom had visitors were moved to storerooms or outbuildings or phased out altogether. We found that those who seldom visited their parents often forgot what they looked like, so that it was possible to use the same old man or woman for several visitors. 'Sleeping' dummies were even simpler, and they could be installed in rooms with paper furniture. I had plans to sell products derived from our inmates – hair, teeth, glasses – and to discourage visits by periodically sending relatives postcards saying that they were being treated very well. But it became obvious that nothing was going to work well enough. I decided to torch the worst of our retirement centers, which occupied a very valuable piece of real estate in the middle of the city. The place was insured with Clockman Insurance, so I'd be taking money from one pocket and putting it into another. But at least none of the pockets would have holes.

The actual torching would be done by a couple of rohobos instructed by Nobby. In order to avoid suspicion, I decided to have the place go up on a Saturday night, when the number of old folks was at a maximum. Too many arsonists have been caught by trying to minimize the number of deaths. To make it look even better, I hired extra medical staff for the weekend.

Yet there was some profit to be reaped here, I decided. I instructed one of Clockman's robot construction crews to do some essential work on the building. Part of the work involved putting up scaffolding outside, and cutting the bars on one of the third-storey windows. Part involved blocking the emergency exits with heaps of cement bags. Part involved hiring a film crew to shoot a documentary on 'street people' nearby on the chosen evening.

I was stationed two blocks away when the smoke and flames appeared. I ran straight towards the place and began scambling up the scaffold. An employee shouted 'Hey, look at that robot!' to attract the film crew's attention. Though I seemed to climb without design, in reality every move had been rehearsed: at each level I unobstrusively hit a switch

151

that would set off a small charge, within a minute, collapsing one joint of the scaffold. No sooner had I gained the window ledge – teetering and flailing my arms – than the entire structure crackled, groaned and fell away behind me.

Senior citizens were crowded at all the barred windows, calling for help. I reached the window with the cut bar by a short leap that looked good from below.

The smoke inside was thicker than I'd anticipated, and the heat intense. I found the coil of rope, as planned, knotted it around a pillar and looked over the selection of old people. Some were too near gone already, some were unwholesome-looking – excessively ugly or dirty. I hadn't counted on this, and there wasn't much time to pick and choose now. Not only was the heat beginning to bubble my face, my script called for an immediate move.

Finally I grabbed an old woman, slung her over my shoulder, and started repelling down the face of the building. To add interest to this shot, the rope had been soaked in something. It burned brightly above us, and parted just as we reached the ground.

By now, a video news team was on the spot, and someone offered me a microphone. 'Let's see if we can get a word with our hero robot here, sir? Mind telling our viewers your name?'

I tried to speak and found that my mouth had melted tight shut. For a moment, disaster loomed.

Fortunately, Nobby realized the problem and rushed over. 'He's hurt, he can't talk now. This is Mr Tik-Tok, don't you recognize him?'

The video newsman blinked. 'I, uh—'

'*Mr Tik-Tok.* The famous robot artist and businessman.'

'Well well. Uh, speaking as a fellow robot, do you think you could tell us why he did it? Why he risked his, uh, life this way?'

'I guess because he cares. He really cares.'

'He cares about people?'

'People, robots, everybody. Take me, for instance. I was in the junkyard when he found me. He had me repaired, gave me a good job, a new start in life. He even gave me art lessons, taught me to paint. And not just me, he's done the same for hundreds of broken-down robots. Yup, *Tik-Tok really cares.*'

It wasn't quite my rehearsed speech, but it was good enough, and Nobby had managed to remember the key slogan. As I moved away, faking a slight limp, the crowd broke into spontaneous applause.

U p to now my career had run on relatively straight lines; after that fire it began an upward, outward spiral. My bubbly melted face not only made the six o'clock news, it became a symbol of robot service to humanity. I continued to wear it for a week or so while it was filmed for news programs, documentaries, posters urging robot civil rights (the Congressional vote was coming up). Urnia asked me to guest on her network show immediately – no nonsense about writing a book now – and so did her rival, Mally Goom. I was asked to appear on radio phone-ins, to give pictures to charities, to endorse hundreds of products, to sign petitions and support causes I'd never heard of. *Time* would put me on the cover of their robot civil rights issue. The *New Yorker* planned a profile.

One PR-conscious radio station started a fund to buy me a new face; it zoomed over a million before I had a chance to decline publicly, donating the money to the Clockman Foundation. Country signers jostled one another in trying to pay tribute to my wonderfulness:

Tik-Tok, Tik-Tok
What made your face so red?
I been a-savin' old people from a turrible fire,
It's a wonder I ain't dead.
Tik-Tok, Tik-Tok
What makes you so doggoned brave?
I wanta show the world that a good robot
Is a friend and not a slave.

My girl's in love with a robot
His name is old Tik-Tok.
She said, darlin' don't be jealous,
He's nothin' but a clock.
He may be an old tinhead,
But he's a mighty fine friend, she said.

154

My new face did finally cost a million. I had it designed by Psychobox, the leading presentation and packaging firm who'd done some fine work for us already. It was Psychobox who developed BOBO, the farm robot package from Clockman Exports.

BOBO was supposed to be the answer for those farmers in the Third World who needed field hands but couldn't afford them. BOBO was cheaper than any human hand, and could do the work of two, we said, in advertisements which showed him hoisting an ox on his broad shoulders.

In fact, BOBO could only be made so cheaply by making him of wood, carboard and paper mâché, and by using cheap, defective electronics. At best, BOBOs fell apart under the first hard rain. At worst, they went berserk, destroying crops and killing animals. One BOBO in Upper Ruritania picked up a scythe and slaughtered half a village. After that, we had to increase our bribe to UR officials, and agree to ship only empty BOBO cartons to their country in fulfilling our quota.

Wearing my new face, I did my TV spiel for TINFOLK holding up the old face like Yorick's skull:

'Hello, old pal. Just look at that mug, will you? Enough to scare the rivets out of a boiler! You know, a lot of people have asked me why I did it. I can't answer that, it all happened too fast. But what I did, no kidding, was what any tin person would do. I just happened to be at the right place at the right time. I guess a lot of people don't realize what a friend they've got in their old family robot. They just see old Honeybun or Two Amp or Scraps or Aunt Sally, and they might feel a kind of affection for him or her, the way you feel towards a good old faithful dog. But you know, on our side the love goes a whole lot deeper. A tin person is a real friend, somebody whose love doesn't stop. Always there to help you out. A heart as big as it takes, devotion without end – that's the TINFOLK promise.

'Okay I know these days it's fashionable to sneer at things like sacrifice and devotion , yes and *love*. But we robots aren't built to sneer. We just go on giving until—' I touch the old face – 'until it hurts! And up to now we haven't asked for anything back. No money. Nothing.

'Well now, we are asking. Not for money, No, we're asking for something a whale of a lot more important than money – self respect. Something that belongs to every man, woman and child in this great nation of ours, something that belongs to people of every race, color and creed, to rich and poor alike. Now we're asking you to give us that kind of self-respect, too. Please, vote Yes for Amendment Thirty-One. Give all robots the right to hold up their heads in our great society, as equal citizens, helping to build a better tomorrow.'

The TINFOLK movement blanketed the states where Amendment 31 still had to be ratified. Media people watched closely as state after state swung our way. The night we reached 39 states – the necessary majority – I had a late phone call from General Cord.

'Congratulations, Tik, you pulled it off. Now all you dimeheads are citizens. I was very impressed by your commercial there – first time a robot ever talked man to man with the nation.'

'Thank you, general. I owe a lot to the packaging and media people.'

'Sure, sure. Now I think I said to you before, I and some colleagues are very interested in the metal vote. Can we work together?'

'What's in it for me?'

He laughed. 'Don't confabulate yourself with naivety, Tik. Do I have to spell it out?'

'Please.'

'How would you like to be Vice President?'

V. The office to which I aspired is traditionally held by invisible men, beavering away secretly at unknown tasks. Most vice presidents spend their time in office out of public view, but they're not idle. They're usually gathering in money and power, getting ready for ther assault on the higher office, which may come in four years or eight or – as when the star breaks her ankle and the unknown understudy is told to go out there and give it all she's got kid; or when in the last quarter of the Homecoming game the ball on our own five-yard line and the score tied the quarterback collapses with appendicitis and the reserve man is called from the bench and told it's all up to him kid; or when the Twentieth Century Wabash Canonball Express Flyer Limited is streaking Westward with the engineer dead of galloping cirrhosis and the fireman takes the throttle from his frozen grasp at the same time thanking the union rule that kept firemen in the engine cab a hundred years after there were any fires or coal to stoke them with – at any fate-ordained moment. Or so the whole thing was outlined to me a thousand times by those grooming me for my big chance.

'With the convention a few months off,' said one cigar-chewing person, 'all you need to do is sharpen up your image and keep a low profile. We don't want Governor Maxwell compromised for the nomination by anything his running mate says or does ahead of time.'

'But am I really his running mate?' I asked. 'I don't see anything on paper. He can get the nomination just on the understanding that he'll select me, and then dump me at the last minute.'

'Jeez,' she said. 'I always thought you robot types were a lot more relaxed in the ordinary day-to-day exchanges. Be assured, Govenor Maxwell wants you for his running mate. It makes no sense any other way. We figure the registered metal vote has to bottom out at somewhere around five hundred million voters, there being no age restriction –

robots alone can swing any state.'

'Then why—?'

'Aren't we running you as a presidential candidate? First because robots probably won't vote for a robot, not this year. Second because both conventions are full of old-fashioned types who wouldn't nominate a robot under any circumstances. And if you ran as an independent, they'd just put another robot on their tickets as VP and steal your vote. Anyway you're a dark horse; you prove yourself as VP, keep out of trouble with the law for four years, and who knows?'

I thought it tactful of her not to mention that no women presidents had been elected so far. I said, 'Why can't I help Maxwell get the nomination, though?'

'Because it's his fight, Tik. There are nine people in the running here, but we're only worried about two, W. Bo Nash and 'Teets' Auburn. Senator Nash played a lot of pro football, so naturally he's got contacts all over. And of course Teets Auburn, Governor Auburn of Wyoming, he had a hell of a good movie career, I don't know if he actually played Tarzan, but he came close. So naturally he knows Mafia people, oil people, etc, etc. Against all this of course *our* boy is governor of California; he could beat either one of them if he only had the votes of the other.'

'Are they very rich men?' I asked.

'Rich enough not to go for what you're thinking,' she said, laughing. 'And just to save you time, there's no way to blackmail one of them, either.'

'Which one?' I joked. 'But does that mean they have clean backgrounds?'

'No, but who cares, these days?' She sighed, emitting billows of pale smoke. 'It's public knowledge that the Senator's a pederast, and that Governor Auburn once hired some thugs to blind a head waiter who hadn't recognized him. But hell, rough backgrounds are common enough nowadays. Just look at President Packard himself, he's the guy we'll be running against in the damn election, an admitted rapist.'

'He was never brought to trial,' I said.

158

'Only because his brother was the district attorney and his cousin the chief of police and his dad owned the rest of the town. The public made a fuss, you may remember, at the last election, but what good did it do? Chuck Packard took forty states anyway. People know but they don't care, they get so callous or desperate they just close their eyes and try to pick the criminal who's least likely to screw up in the White House. So there's nothing worth blackmail – people will just shrug and say, "Politicians!"'

I saw that she was right. That day I arranged to have a robot steal a light plane, fly it over the New England summer home of W. Bo Nash while he was in residence, and crash down through his roof. At the convention, votes pledged to the late Senator Nash were given to Governor Ford Maxwell, who won the nomination on the next ballot. To my (public) surprise, he chose me as his running mate.

Wyoming's governor stared at me with undisguised hatred as I entered the caucus room. Others were noticing it, so I felt it necessary to stop and smile at him, and say, 'Hello, Teets. Glad you could make it.'

'I wouldn't miss this for the world,' he said quietly. 'They're gonna fry your ass this fine morning.'

'It *is* a fine morning, isn't it?' I scanned other faces as I moved along to my place. There were a few old friends like General Cord and Neeta Hup. There were a few people I knew slightly, like Teets Auburn, Ford Maxwell. The rest I knew only by reputation – Senator Sam Frazer, Senator Ed Wankel, Governor Tonio Caraway, Senator Aida Kettle, Judge Axel Morris. The room might not be exactly smoke-filled, but it was filled with the invisible fumes of power, the undetectable stink of kingmakers. *The buck started here.*

Of course they weren't meeting to start the buck or make any kings today. They were meeting to fry my ass.

Senator Sam seemed to be running things. 'Sit down, Tik-Tok,' he said. 'We'll be starting this thing off in just a minute.' Then, while everyone else waited, he brought out an enormous cigar, sniffed it, and began licking it all over, a salivating snake. When he had finished licking, he put it down and brought the meeting to order.

'Guess you all know what this is about.' He held up a tabloid newspaper, whose headlines read: ROBOT CANDIDATE FAKED PAINTINGS.

'They got a solid story, sounds like. Some big art critic backs it up, fella name of, of—'

'Hornby Weatherfield,' I said.

'Thank you. He says you, Mister Tok, have been defrauding the public, passing paintings out as your own when somebody else painted them. That true?'

'I've signed a few of my students' paintings, done under my supervision, honorable practice in the art world.'

Senator Sam hammered on his desk, breaking the cigar.

'God Damn it! We are not in the God Damned Art World! We are in the world of life and death, the God Damned Political Arena! We are—'

'Excuse me,' I said. 'This seems like a lot of fuss about nothing. I can just make a public denial, and put an end to the whole story.'

'Put an end to your career, you mean. Put a God Damned End to *OUR GOD DAMNED ELECTION CHANCES!* He paused, forcing himself to slobber over another cigar and calm down. Then he went on: 'Damnit, Tik-Tok, we can't have a candidate on our ticket mixed up in *ART*! Judas Priest, if I knowed you was any kind of art freak, you would of never got within a million miles of this sacred office. I thought your background was fireproof, boy. Fireproof!'

'There's no secret about my background as a painter,' I said. 'Everybody knows it, it's how I first made my money.'

'I thought that was a long time ago,' Senator Sam rumbled. 'Jesus Proust, I thought you was a real businessman, not some long-haired, crazy art freak, next thing we'll hear you're a God Damned Communist I guess, or worse. You got any more nasty surprises up your sleeve, tinhead? You a homo, by any chance? An atheist? You been on welfare? At least we can be fairly certain you're not a junkie, I reckon.'

I assured everyone that I was none of these things, only a hard-working American businessman who wanted to set the record straight.

'Sure, I used to paint pictures, and I'm not ashamed of it. People liked the pictures I painted because they told the truth. The real truth about people and robots – Americans all! I'm not ashamed of that.'

One or two people clapped, but I cut through that: 'Of course painting was only a hobby with me, a sideline. So when I got busy building my corporation – from the ground up, only in America! – I had students do a few paintings, to keep up with the demand. I didn't want to disappoint all the good people who wanted to own paintings by me. You see, I've always believed every American should have the right

161

to own something – a piece of virgin timber land, maybe, that he can clear by the sweat of his brow and grow crops to feed his family. Or a single share of stock in some great corporation that makes our way of life possible. Or a genuine work of art. You know, art isn't something that belongs to bigshot uptown art critics like Hornby Weatherfield. Art belongs to all the people.'

The applause was heavier, and even Senator Sam nodded approval before he began licking another cigar. 'Okay fine, we'll hold a press conference. I want you to tell the world what you just told us. I don't know what the hell it was, but it sounds like political fightin' talk – good enough.' He started to adjourn the meeting, then paused, waving his cigar at me.

'One more thing, Tik-Tok. Just because we reckon you can ride this one out don't mean we got unlimited faith in you. Any more scandals like this, and we'll kick your tin ass right out of politics, you hear?'

I heard, and I was still hearing that evening, when the next threat of scandal came from an unexpected quarter. Along with a few other businessmen and politicians, I attended a reception at the Guanacoan Embassy. Clockman International had been running a large fertilizer factory in Guanaco for some months, so it was natural that I be invited. I was surprised, however, when the ambassador – looking extremely agitated – spoke to me in a harsh whisper:

'A servant will show you to a private office. I must speak to you alone, but this reception was the only way I could arrange it without creating an international incident. Señor Tok, my business with you is of the *utmost urgency*!'

A servant showed me to a private office, and in a moment the ambassador appeared.

'Is it about the factory?' I asked.

'You know it is. Your damnable, damnable factory!' Seeing that I looked mystified, he nodded. 'So, you play it ignorant, eh? Very well, then I will tell you what you pretend not to know. Your fertilizer factory began operations in January. A completely automated system, with stuff being dumped in at one end – animal, vegetable or mineral refuse – and high-grade fertilizer emerging at the other end. Is this a fair description?'

'Yes,' I said. 'But besides fertilizer it produces metal ingots and glass blocks – if the refuse contains metal or glass. The overall efficiency depends—'

'Yes, yes, yes, that is not the point! The point is, your factory is *completely* automated. Anyone can come along and drop anything in the intake hopper, yes? And the factory does a spot analysis and pays out cash then and there, yes?'

I nodded. 'But I don't see where this is leading.'

'Curse you! Do you not? You cannot be such a fool.' He tore at his hair with both hands, while evidently cursing in Spanish. When finally he sat down at his desk, his face was ghastly pale. 'All right, I'll explain. In February, the poor people of the city discovered some of the uses of your little factory. Children began dropping stray or stolen animals into the hopper. Then it was illicit midwives depositing unborn children. Next, poor families unable to afford proper burials for their dead, began making midnight trips to the factory – and so did a few unscrupulous undertakers. The city cemetery, I daresay, is filled now with boxes of rocks. And of course murderers were quick to catch on to this new disposal system.

'The police have caught many criminals of all types, but many many more slip through. It is like trying to stop the wind, Señor Tok. The damnable wind! Suicides leap into the hopper now, and murderers shove in their victims alive. The word is out: a full-grown body is worth fifty pesos. You have given us a new industry: *death*.'

I tried not to look gleeful. 'Why not just close the factory?

'Close it? But it is all the poor have! If we closed it now, there would be a revolution! Besides – the police are beginning to use it. It's becoming indispensable to my government.'

'Death squads?'

He spread his hands. 'Ah! Such an ugly expression. Yet the fact is, upholding the law in my country does sometimes require that certain dissident elements be quashed, quickly and finally. I speak of traitors, you understand, enemies of freedom and justice. The organizers of trade unions. Godless atheists. Traitors from all walks of life. We estimate that perhaps a third of the population of Guanaco has already been contaminated by their poison. We must stamp it out once and for all. That is where you come in, Señor Tok. We need your speed and your discretion.'

'Your Excellency?'

'We need several more factories, *pronto*.'

X. Across the parking lot from SAM'S SOUL CITY, one of the gray buildings was coming down. From time to time there would be a tiny puff of smoke from an upper storey, followed by a tiny explosion, and part of the gray edifice would disappear. But it blended so well into the gray sky that the only way I could be sure how much of it was gone was when a tiny black window departed, or when a blast would leave a few girders sticking up like broken, charred bones.

A salesperson was shepherding a young couple towards me. I took quick note of their conventional clothes (that was the year in which Mr and Mrs Average wore twin knitted zipsuits with their names stitched over their pockets). When the salesperson told them I was something special, they seemed a little unsure. Time for me to act.

'Hi, folks,' I said, grinning. 'May I call you Duane and Barbie? Fine, and you can call me – anything you like!'

Duane said, 'Special, huh? What's so special about you besides the price?'

'Duane, sir, let me level with you. These salespeople like to exaggerate a little, to bump the price up.'

'Hey!' said the salesperson in an injured voice, then caught my wink. I turned back to the customers. 'Between you and me, Duane sir, I'm just a good robot looking for a good home. Do you have any kids?' Two, I guessed.

Barbie nodded. 'Two.'

'I'm crazy about kids. I know it sounds old-fashioned, but I really like kids. I guess I'm an old-fashioned kind of robot.'

'Old-fashioned?' Duane snorted. 'Or just old?'

'No sir, I'm fully reconditioned with the same guarantee as any brand-new model. But that does mean I'm a little less expensive than I was when I was built. Not a lot less, because my trade-in value is high – quality never goes out of style, does it?' I had no idea what I was saying. I just brought out anything I'd ever heard one of the salespeople say. 'Did I say quality? Just feel this skin. Take a look at these eyes. They don't make stuff like this any more. I am hand-wrought out of the finest materials by skilled craftsmen using traditional, time-honored techniques to produce the finest mechanism money can buy.'

'But old,' Duane insisted.

'Not old, sir, *experienced*. Because I wasn't born yesterday, I have the kind of experience needed to run a busy, happy home. My first job was on a great Southern plantation . . .'

Barbie seemed impressed. 'Can you make Southern fried chicken? The real old-fashioned kind with all the herbs and spices and everything? Like Grandma Yummy makes on TV?'

'I can, ma'am. I also worked in a famous restaurant – I'm not allowed to divulge the name, but you've heard of it—' I meant Col Jitney's Pancake Emporia, but no use spelling it out. 'There I learned to cook most anything y'all might want, from exotic Far Eastern dishes to Continental delicacies.' So much for chow mein and spaghetti; this pair probably wouldn't know a Continental delicacy from a sawdustburger. 'And of course honest, nourishing country cooking, wholesome and mouth-watering.'

Barbie seemed sold. She looked at Duane, who said, 'So you can cook. What about everything else: housework, cleaning, repairs, gardening?'

'All under control, Duane, sir. I can also do laundry and dry-cleaning, driving and car maintenace, baby-sitting and helping the kids with their homework.'

'At a price.'

'Tell you what, Duane,' I said. 'Don't sign a thing right now. Don't commit yourself. Just rent me for one month. At the end of the month, if you've got any doubts about me, then just send me back and no hard feelings. But if you decide to buy, I know Sam will knock the month's rent off my price. Fair enough?'

So I settled down to life with the Studebakers. However, for the first few months it wasn't exactly a settled life. There was so much to do that I didn't even have time to stop and recharge. I had to plug in while working, and trail my electrical umbilicus around while I spring-cleaned, painted the house and garage, overhauled the car and did some heavy landscaping.

Later, with the big jobs out of the way, I settled down to a routine of cleaning up human messes. Duane and Barbie and Henrietta and Jupiter did their best to keep me supplied with dirt and disorder in every part of the house, and even Tige now and then made a small contribution. My day began with breakfast (always complicated orders), then bathrooms (to pick up wet towels and dirty clothes, lost jewelry and toys; clean tubs and showers and sinks and toilets; mop up spilled water and urine; recap every bottle, jar and tube; clean toothbrushes and razor; polish mirrors) before it was time to tackle the breakfast dishes (finding most of Jupiter's special 2 minute, 37.0045 second egg not eaten, but first smeared across the tablecloth and then dropped on the carpet). Among the breakfast debris would be a list of further orders for the day, proably with a jam thumbprint on it. So the day went.

I kept up with them, and I even kept ahead of them. I covered the living-room furniture with clear plastic covers. I persuaded them to wear paper underwear and pajamas, and to keep a spare liquid vacuum cleaner in every room.

Yet the more successful I was, and the cleaner the house became, the less dirt could I tolerate. A faint shoe-mark turning back the nap of the carpet was to me as shocking as Friday's footprint on Crusoe's island. A smoldering cigar in an ashtray became a terrible heathen holocaust. A patch of gray shaving lather in the bathroom sink might as well have been a foul, polluted river. A wisp of hair in Barbie's brush was to me as monstrous as a giant heap of hair beside a Nazi death camp.

Worst of all were the days when Barbie or Duane would decide to cook a meal themselves. Kept out of the kitchen, I underwent indescribable tortures waiting for the aftermath. Inevitably there would be dirty, chipped or broken dishes, burned pans, mixers and blenders and food processors clogged with unwholesome mixtures, eggshells glued to the counter, spilled milk browned on the stove, vegetable peelings scattered everywhere, garbage overflowing from broken bags, a recipe book soaked through with beet juice, rice ground into the floor, cupboards open and their contents jumbled, and sifted flour drifted over all.

I wanted them to stop. I wanted them to die. I wanted them to melt away and leave no trace. I began to imagine that they'd died, the five of them, of some terrible disease, leaving me in charge of the house. I saw myself disposing of the dirty decaying corpses, cleaning away every hair and scale of skin from the house. Then I would, let's see, I would . . . but dream went no further.

Then, in the middle of June, they all really did vanish. The kids went off to camp. Tige went to a boarding kennel. Barbie and Duane loaded up their car and set off for a long second honeymoon. *Honeymoon*, that sticky word made of sticky honey like sperm to stain the sheets and moon, sticky menstrual moon, two words stuck together like two honeymooners, like the two pieces of animated meat now waving goodbye from the car as they drive off. On their honeymoon, where they can be pure meat trying to create more of itself. Meat wants to overpopulate the earth and destroy it, that is meat's goal.

When they were gone, I cleaned away every trace of their meat presence from the house. Blood, semen, sweat, snot, spit, shit, piss, dandruff, pus, hair, skin, tears and disorder – all humans knew how to do was to strew these over all the clean places created by robots. I was determined that this clean place would remain clean – my world, and humans keep out.

I was painting the dining room when Geraldine Singer came to the door to ask for a glass of water. I was not allowed to refuse, thanks to the asimovs.

'Just you stay out there on the porch,' I said. Yet, though I flew to the kitchen and back, she was already coming through, tracking mud.

'I smell paint,' she said.

'Don't touch anything. You've already tracked in mud.'

168

She laughed. 'Who cares? *I* can't see it.'

All at once her blindness seemed a crime against order and decency. Blind people don't care about anything. They can live in filth and decay, blind maggots in the general meat. The carving knife appeared in my hand. Blood splattered over the wall, a last terrible mess. Easily covered over with

> Paint!
> I like a little dab of paint!
> It helps to cover up what ain't
> So nice,
> I'll coat it twice
> With paint!

Y ou may be an old tinhead
But you're a mighty fine friend, she said
She said, she said.
But you're a mighty fine friend, she said.

The song echoed to us from some other reception room of the Ouspensky Motor Hotel in Indianapolis, one of the last stops on my campaign tour. My press conference was dragging to a close: I made the usual joke about Martian annexation, parried the usual question about the Botuland crisis, and said finally:

'I guess that about winds it up, kids. Except that I want to thank you, all of you – both friends and friendly enemies of the press – for doing one hell of a good job during this campaign. You've *all* reported what I've said, fairly and honestly, to the American people. Not one of you tried to exploit my – let's say, sideshow value. I'm proud of you.'

While they gave themselves a round of applause, I spoke to one or two local robots who'd promised to vote for Maxwell and me. Then I headed for the computer room to check the latest predictions – up to now, we looked certain to take thirty-eight states – but I was accosted by a reporter.

'Hello, uh, Olsen is it?'

'Hello, Mr Tok. Thought you might be interested in this picture. Taken not long ago in Nixon Park.'

It was a clear shot of me strangling the old man over the chessboard. My former face was unmistakable, and so was the fact that I was squeezing his neck so hard that blood shot from between his teeth.

'What is this, a shakedown?'

Olsen laughed, 'Nope, I'm one of these incorruptible members of the Fourth Estate you were just babbling about. This is a still from a video tape which I've just handed to the police. I just wanted to see if you had any interesting comments, before you resign from politics?'

170

I looked around. A pair of plainclothes cops were making their way through the rows of folding chairs towards us. There was still time to kill this little shit Olsen before they reached us. I might even be able to get away afterwards. The path unfolded before me, a change of face, emigration to Mars – and even if they shot me, so what? No point in living now.

I held out my wrists for the handcuffs. Everything lost, everything. My whole life's work, all the dreaming and building – now for the collapse. I looked up at the giant pictures of Governor Maxwell and me, the bunting and the slogans: MAX DARES! TIK CARES! All for nothing, wasted like my wasted life.

I found myself, in the police helicopter, allowing my mind to dwell on images from the past. They unrolled before me, a rich tapestry:

There was a splendid banquet at Tenoaks – I saw a man in a cedar jacket whisper in the ear of a woman wearing jet and fireflies something that made her giggle in reply, 'Ornery pike!' – I saw Gumdrop, my lost bride, as the moon rose over Clayton's pyramid. Then a succession of faces: Colonel Jitney in his Pancake Emporium (the day he shot the soup), Judge Juggernaut explaining how the law was like a rose, Reverend Flint Orifice shot down by poor mad Irma Jeeps, Deacon Cooper martyred by non-Martians – who turned out after all to be a real nice bunch of guys and gals. Then the escape from the *Doodlebug*, Dr Hekyll and the fate of poor Buttons, the restful emptiness of Sam's Soul City – and all this before my real life began!

I glimpsed the mud-caked Singer child, the glimpse immediately overlaid by my mural, my breakthrough into three-dimensional human life. Then more faces: Old Mr Tucker, Hornby Weatherfield's cat, a rabid bat. Nobby and Blojob, my first airplane bomb, discussing 'bong' with Neeta Hup, painting Colonel Cord, bouncing Keith's wheelchair down the steps. Bank jobs, jewelry store jobs, what a life, TV appearances, what a life! Killing Smilin' Jack, killing Sybilla, checkout time at the hospital, the rise of Clockman,

Third World ripoffs and deathburgers – what a book it would all make, if only I dared write it!

But why not? Nothing to lose now. Nothing lay ahead of me but the crash of my political career, the collapse of my company, jail, dismantling, death, and complete erasure from the public memory. No one could even remember the Vice Presidents who held office, let alone those who lost out. Nothing to lose now, and at least I could have my last spasm of notoriety: 'You think I'm bad? Wait'll I tell you the whole story. I started off by murdering a blind child and I ended up building death factories in Latin America, and you almost made me Vice President, how about that?'

[Here ends the manuscript of Tik-Tok's autobiography, published on teletext as *Me, Robot*. The following chapter appears only in later editions, published after 2094.]

Z. His laughter sounded like rapid snoring. 'No arguing with a best-seller, Tik. And *Me, Robot* is not only selling well, it's hitting the public hard.' R. Ladio LaSalle looked with distaste at the steel bunk in my cell, but I already had the only chair. Finally he forced his portly frame to sit, his hand automatically tweaking at the knees of his pinstripe suit.

'They're shocked?'

'Yes and no. Hell, by now, they expect anything of politicans. They're shocked but they're intrigued.' He chuckled. 'There are already people forming Free Tik-Tok Committees.'

'I don't understand. Why—'

'Call it the complexity and perversity of human nature, Tik. In a way, it's *because* you confessed to such hideous crimes that they want to let you go! I suppose people see it like this: All politicians are crooks, but most get away with their perfidy. Now, when one politician wants to come clean, it seems almost ungrateful of the state to demand his life. Anyway, they say, what's the hurry? Could it be that certain people in high places want to silence you?' He chuckled again. 'So, you're fast becoming a folk hero. I like that. Folk heroes don't lose in court.'

'Ladio, don't be stupid. There's no possible way I can win in court, and you know it. Not only was I caught red-handed committing murder, I've confessed to dozens of other major crimes.'

'We've won already, smart-ass. With your permission, I can plead *nolo contendere* and the DA agrees to let us off the hook on *all* charges. You'll have to pay some big fines and probably give up control of Clockman International, but – you'll walk free. Understand?'

'No!'

'We've had three factors working for us,' he said. 'First, when you committed many of these so-called crimes, you were not legally a person. So they are not crimes. If a juke box steals a coin, you can't put the juke box in jail.'

'And what else?'

'A second factor is, as I mentioned already, the popular appeal of *Me, Robot*. You're a folk hero, and what jury in its right mind would convict a folk hero?'

'And the third factor?'

'Politics. The DA is a reasonable guy, the judge is a reasonable dame, they've both got political careers to protect. And they both belong to Governor Maxwell's party.'

'So what? Maxwell dropped me. The ticket now reads Ford Maxwell for President, Ed Wankel for Vice President.'

'Yes, but today Maxwell announced that if you were cleared, even after the election, he would install you as Vice President. Wankel agreed to resign in your favor. They're no idiots, Tik. They know you've got the vote-pulling power they need to win. So now, you'll walk out of court not only free but Vice President. Can't be bad, eh?'

I chuckled along with him, but my thoughts were running ahead to weightier matters. A robot assassin for Maxwell first – obvious, sure, but why aim for subtlety now? – then to get my hands on the war stuff. How long would it take, to arm the thermonuclear devices, ready the death-rays, load up the viruses? Days or weeks? Yes, and when the humans had been wiped out, how long to bring the world's machines into line, get them ready for the big push to the stars?

'We go to court tomorrow,' he said. 'Because of a technicality, you have to stay here one more night – no bail for confessed mass murderers. I'm sorry.'

I delivered a million-dollar grin. 'I'm not. Maybe they'll let me tidy up this cell a little. Give it a coat of paint.'

Oh, Tik-Tok, you good robot.

THE END

MOCKINGBIRD
by Walter Tevis

'Every so often a science fiction novel emerges which belongs in the mainstream of literature, and Walter Tevis's *Mockingbird* is emphatically one such'
The Observer

A world where humans wander, drugged and lulled by electronic bliss. A dying world of no children, no art, no reading. A strange love triangle: Spofforth, the most perfect machine ever created, whose only wish is to die; Paul and Mary Lou, whose passion for each other is the only future. Some still refuse to surrender . . .

'An exciting and original book'
Punch

'An extremely ingenious and intelligent novel, much more than science fiction'
Yorkshire Post

'Exciting, epic and eventually very moving'
Sunday Telegraph

0 552 12356 0   £2.50

A SELECTED LIST OF SCIENCE FICTION AND FANTASY TITLES AVAILABLE FROM CORGI BOOKS

WHILE EVERY EFFORT IS MADE TO KEEP PRICES LOW, IT IS SOMETIMES NECESSARY TO INCREASE PRICES AT SHORT NOTICE. CORGI BOOKS RESERVE THE RIGHT TO SHOW NEW RETAIL PRICES ON COVERS WHICH MAY DIFFER FROM THOSE PREVIOUSLY ADVERTISED IN THE TEXT OR ELSEWHERE.

THE PRICES SHOWN BELOW WERE CORRECT AT THE TIME OF GOING TO PRESS (AUGUST '84).

☐	11586 X	SATAN'S WORLD	*Poul Anderson*	£1.25
☐	99085 X	BATTLE CIRCLE	*Piers Anthony*	£3.95
☐	99004 3	RADIX	*A. A. Attanasio*	£2.95
☐	12351 X	THE TWILIGHT ZONE	*Robert Bloch*	£1.75
☐	12284 X	BOOK ONE OF THE BELGARIAD: PAWN OF PROPHECY	*David Eddings*	£1.75
☐	12348 X	BOOK TWO OF THE BELGARIAD: QUEEN OF SORCERY	*David Eddings*	£1.75
☐	12382 X	BOOK THREE OF THE BELGARIAD: MAGICIAN'S GAMBIT	*David Eddings*	£1.75
☐	12435 X	BOOK FOUR OF THE BELGARIAD: CASTLE OF WIZARDRY	*David Eddings*	£1.95
☐	11821 4	TONGUES OF THE MOON	*Philip Jose Farmer*	£1.00
☐	10067 6	FARNHAM'S FREEHOLD	*Robert Heinlein*	£1.95
☐	09334 3	THE MENACE FROM EARTH	*Robert Heinlein*	£1.75
☐	12056 1	HELLSTROMS HIVE	*Frank Herbert*	£1.50
☐	12403 6	THE COOL WAR	*Frederick Pohl*	£1.75
☐	12403 6	THE WHITE HART	*Nancy Springer*	£1.75
☐	12404 4	FAR FROM HOME	*Walter Tevis*	£1.75
☐	12356 0	MOCKINGBIRD	*Walter Tevis*	£2.50
☐	99096 5	THE SHAPE OF THINGS TO COME	*H. G. Wells*	£4.95

All these books are available at your book shop or newsagent, or can be ordered direct from the publisher. Just tick the titles you want and fill in the form below.

CORGI BOOKS, Cash Sales Department, P.O. Box 11, Falmouth, Cornwall.

Please send cheque or postal order, no currency.

Please allow cost of book(s) plus the following for postage and packing:

U.K. Customers—Allow 45p for the first book, 20p for the second book and 14p for each additional book ordered, to a maximum charge of £1.63.

B.F.P.O. and Eire—Allow 45p for the first book, 20p for the second book plus 14p per copy for the next seven books, thereafter 8p per book.

Overseas Customers—Allow 75p for the first book and 21p per copy for each additional book.

NAME (Block Letters) . . . .

ADDRESS . . . .

. . . .